A VICTORIAN NATURALIST

Beatrix Potter's Drawings from the Armitt Collection

A VICTORIAN NATURALIST

Beatrix Potter's Drawings from the Armitt Collection

Eileen Jay, Mary Noble, Anne Stevenson Hobbs

F. WARNE & Co

FREDERICK WARNE

Published by the Penguin Group
27 Wrights Lane, London W8 5TZ, England
Penguin Books USA Inc., 375 Hudson Street, New York, N.Y. 10014, USA
Penguin Books Australia Ltd, Ringwood, Victoria, Australia
Penguin Books Canada Ltd, 10 Alcorn Avenue, Toronto, Ontario, Canada M4V 3B
Penguin Books (N.Z.) Ltd, 182–190 Wairau Road, Auckland 10, New Zealand

Penguin Books Ltd, Registered Offices: Harmondsworth, Middlesex, England

First published 1992
1 3 5 7 9 10 8 6 4 2

ISBN 0 7232 3990 8

Designed by Ron Callow

Printed and bound in Great Britain by
William Clowes Limited, Beccles and London

British Library Cataloguing in Publication Data available

CONTENTS

ACKNOWLEDGEMENTS

The publishers would like to thank the following for assistance in preparing this book: John Gavin, Chairman of the Armitt Trust; Dr Roy Watling and the Cryptogamic Botany staff at the Royal Botanic Garden Edinburgh; Dr R. F. O. Kemp; Cressida Pemberton-Pigott for original photographs; Susan Allan; Dr Daniel Altmann; Anne Stevenson Hobbs for her additional work in research and indexing.

ILLUSTRATION ACKNOWLEDGEMENTS

The Beatrix Potter watercolours and other pictures from the Armitt Collection are reproduced by permission of the Trustees.

Additional illustrations are reproduced by permission of the following: (numbers refer to the plates)

Abbot Hall Art Gallery, Kendal, 3
National Art Library, Victoria and Albert Museum, 25, 27, 37, 133, 170, 171, 173, 175, 179, 189, 219, 227, 228
Cressida Pemberton-Pigott, 7, 40, 45
Charlotte Mason College of Education, Ambleside, 18
Private collections, 22, 23, 38, 41, 66, 72, 122
Royal Botanic Gardens, Kew, 36, 116, 119
Richard Satterthwaite Fowkes, 39
Collingwood family, 49
Frederick Warne & Co., 56, 58, 59, 168, 177, 178
Perth and Kinross District Council Museum and Art Gallery Department, 67
National Library of Scotland, 71, 109, 138
Royal Botanic Garden Edinburgh, 118
National Trust, 163, 195
Rare Book Department, Free Library of Philadelphia, 172, 176, 183, 221

BEATRIX POTTER AND THE ARMITT COLLECTION
by Eileen Jay

Foreword

Beatrix Potter – artist, writer, amateur scientist, Lakeland sheep farmer, and National Trust benefactor – became a member of the Armitt Library shortly after her marriage to William Heelis in 1913. Many years later she gave the Armitt Trust hundreds of her natural history watercolour drawings, mainly of fungi, together with microscope studies, archaeological paintings, and books: an important part of her scientific studies little known until long after her death.

Today, the various other collections of this remarkable woman's work are housed in some of London's main museums and art galleries, and by the National Trust in the Lake District. The Armitt Trust's Beatrix Potter collection in Ambleside is just one of the larger collections, though unique in a significant way. It is the only public collection given by the artist herself.

At first sight it seems strange that this specialised collection, once so close to her heart and early ambitions, should have been given to a small, and then little-known trust. The following brief account of the Armitt Library and the three sisters who made it all possible, may perhaps go some way to showing how this came about.

THE ARMITT LIBRARY

The roots of the Armitt Collection were formed long before the library's official opening in 1912. They grew out of a remarkable group of active and gifted people who, in the nineteenth century, were living in the Ambleside area.

Perhaps at that time in the English Lake Country the unspoiled natural beauty, sparse population and slower pace of life in the quiet of the hills encouraged life to be lived at a more profound level than usual. Certainly, and for whatever reason, the creativity of Wordsworth, the Arnolds of Fox How, Thomas de Quincey, Harriet Martineau, Ruskin, and various other writers, artists, and social reformers was flourishing there. Also active were educational pioneers like Anne Jemima Clough, the first Principal of Newnham College, Cambridge, W. E. Forster, the Liberal statesman famous for the 1870

1. Windermere, Ambleside, painted by J.B. Pyne in 1851.

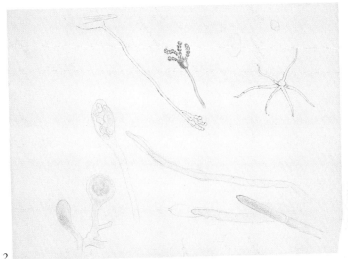

2

3

Education Act which founded a national system of schools, and later, Charlotte M. Mason, the founder of the Parents' National Educational Union, whose teachings and philosophy of education attracted international interest and admiration. Anne Jemima Clough (sister of the poet Arthur Hugh Clough) had earlier opened a school in her Ambleside home, Eller How, where she experimented in teaching methods, and where one of her pupils was the fiery young Mary Arnold who later became the famous Victorian novelist, Mrs Humphrey Ward.

Years later, but long before the provision of provincial record offices, many rare books, manuscripts, pictures, old prints, and personal possessions of such individuals were saved for posterity by being given to the Armitt Library. They reflected the special ambience of those earlier days, and ranged from curios like Wordsworth's picnic carrier and rushlight holder, the life casts of Harriet Martineau's face and hands and a lock of Ruskin's hair, to Beatrix Potter's microscope drawings (including a study of an organism 'on a fly's foot in water'), rare books like Redouté's *Les Roses*, Camden's *Britannia* and an early example of printing, a first edition of a missal printed in Basle in 1509.

The Armitt Library was founded as a subscription library under the will of Mary Louisa Armitt, and in

2. Sheet of microscope drawings by Beatrix Potter including an organism 'on a fly's foot in water'.

3. Portrait of Mary Louisa Armitt by Fred Yates. (The artist Fred Yates discovered Rydal when he was commissioned to portray Charlotte Mason in 1901. He decided to live there and subsequently painted many prominent Lakeland residents.)

4

4. The Reading Room at Chetham's Library, Manchester, painted by Sophia Armitt in 1891.

accordance with the wishes of her two sisters 'to create a collection of books of scientific, literary or antiquarian value for the student and book-lover'. She left an endowment, together with her books and those of her late sister Sophia, to form the nucleus of a reference library. At the opening in 1912, the Chairman of the Trustees, Willingham Franklin Rawnsley, explained that though some works of fiction would be available for loan, it had not been Miss Armitt's wish to provide 'a free library . . . of the Carnegie type'. She herself had enjoyed researching in reference libraries both at home and abroad, and these included places like Oxford's Bodleian Library, the famous old Chetham's Library in Manchester, and the Royal Library in Brussels. Knowing of the current increase in the provision of public lending libraries, she wished to found an additional facility for students and scholars. Anyone was free to join the library on introduction by a member and the payment of a small subscription. And, as befitted a local historian of no mean distinction, the founder also expressed a wish that the library might include a small museum of local provenance.

5. Hardwicke Rawnsley by Fred Yates.

From the beginning the library embodied the earlier Ambleside Ruskin Library, founded in 1882 under the presidency of Hardwicke D. Rawnsley, a younger brother of Willingham, the first Armitt Library Chairman. Hardwicke was then vicar of Wray Castle church and later became a Canon of Carlisle Cathedral. He had been a Ruskin disciple from his Oxford days when, as an undergraduate, he had joined in the manual work on Professor Ruskin's Hinksey Road project, and Ruskin himself had approved of Rawnsley's Ambleside Library, whose object was 'to promote the study and circulation of Mr Ruskin's Writings and kindred works'. He donated various items and a fine box of geological specimens.

All former Ruskin subscribers became Armitt members in 1912. As well as the Rawnsley brothers, they included Charlotte Mason, Gordon G. Wordsworth, the poet's grandson who became a permanent member of the Armitt Library Committee, and Herbert Bell, the former Ruskin Librarian who continued to serve as Honorary Armitt Librarian.

6. Bust of John Ruskin by Barbara Collingwood.

In 1913, the Armitt Library was presented with the records and assets of a much older institution: the Ambleside Book Society, founded in 1828, and whose membership had included that of Wordsworth. The system then practised can be glimpsed in a letter from his daughter Dora to Edward Quillinan in January 1829:

> My father is a subscriber to a book club in Ambleside what think you of the march of intellect in this northern clime? Exceedingly interested in the book we are now reading – Gen[1] Miller's Memoirs – the worst is we are only allowed seven days for a volume, which makes it a hurry scurrying business, and we can only half enjoy an interesting book when we have it – It does not suit our Poet at all – When he is at work he cannot read, so he has petitioned to be allowed to keep the book beyond the time and pay his fine . . .

The Armitt Library however differed from the old book club in being a reference library, and from the beginning the students from Charlotte Mason's 'House of Education' were given special facilities.

Beatrix Potter became an Armitt Library member in 1913 when she settled in the Lake District after her marriage to William Heelis, also an Armitt member and in addition a trustee. Friends and acquaintances of hers who also subscribed included Rebekah Owen of Belmount near Hawkshead, an American friend of the novelist Thomas Hardy and an authority on his work; and the Windermere philanthropist W. G. Groves, whose property Holehird had been leased by Beatrix's father for the summer in 1889.

Later membership was wide and varied. It ranged from young students and book-lovers to distinguished writers, artists, novelists, poets, Wordsworth scholars, historians, scientists and archaeologists, and a few individuals of more esoteric bent. These included a well-known Kew plant-hunter who explored the dangerous Kansu-Tibet border in the Himalayas, a philosopher, a diplomat, a biblical scholar, and a colonial administrator, all of whom lived in or near Ambleside.

Over the years the Armitt Collection grew by both gift and purchase. Choice items were acquired from other well-known private libraries and institutions as well as by individual gifts, so that the library now contains many unusual and valuable deposits which could not be collected today.

The true spirit and development of the Armitt Library as an educational charity can only be understood if seen within the context of Ruskin-inspired social aims, Charlotte Mason's educational philosophy, and conservation movements. So many of the early Armitt members were involved in good causes, like the saving of the Borrans Field Roman fort site for the nation (page 49).

Hardwicke Rawnsley served on educational committees and was an admirer of Charlotte Mason, who strongly believed that nature study was an important part of education. His public work was wide and varied, and he is particularly remembered now for the special part he played in helping to found the National Trust, the body set up to preserve 'Places of Historic Interest and Natural Beauty'. His energy and enthusiasm were phenomenal, and he had the help of a talented and supportive wife. He often had to suffer

7. Holehird, Windermere, today, photographed by Cressida Pemberton-Pigott.

7

8. Portinscale Bridge painted by Sophia Armitt.

ridicule from the opposition, but fortunately had a sense of humour. After his victory in saving the picturesque Portinscale Bridge from demolition in 1913, he enjoyed repeating the story of how a complete stranger had told him that but for 'that devil Rawnsley' the case for demolition would have been won!

Annie Maria Armitt, sister of the founder, was also an active conservation campaigner. Writing from her home near Manchester in 1883, a whole decade before the National Trust was formed, she caused a stir with a topical article in the London magazine *Modern Thought* entitled 'The Destruction of Natural Scenery in Great Britain'. It touched on Lakeland problems, and was probably inspired by one of Hardwicke's clarion calls to the press for which he was becoming famous.

Beatrix Potter was then only seventeen. Her contribution still lay in the future when she became one of the outstanding benefactors of the National Trust.

THE ARMITT SISTERS

In the preface to Mary L. Armitt's history *Rydal*, published posthumously in 1916, W. F. Rawnsley wrote: 'I question if since the days of the Brontës in the parsonage at Haworth, any small roof-tree ever covered so interesting a triad.'

Certainly the three sisters, Sophia (1847–1908), Annie Maria (1850–1933), and Mary Louisa (1851–1911), obscure Victorian ladies of modest income and poor health, achieved a great deal. Largely self–taught, all three became published writers of surprising range and depth. Sophia, the artist, became an expert botanist and amateur scientist; Annie Maria wrote short stories, novels and poetry, but is best remembered for her trenchant articles on topical subjects like conservation and anti–vivisection (the latter praised by the poet Robert Browning), whilst Mary Louisa, always known as Louie to family and friends, became a polymath in the best Victorian tradition. The shyest and most gentle of the sisters, she was a musician, ornithologist keenly interested in all nature study, historian and antiquarian who wrote books and erudite papers on these and other subjects.

9. Sophia Armitt by Fred Yates.

9

To appreciate the sisters' story we have to do the almost impossible and somehow project ourselves from the present stimulating but fast–moving, noise–polluted and stressful space age, into a less populated world of slow communications and long imposed silences: conditions which, in spite of many hardships, encouraged quiet meditation and creative thought. It was the world Beatrix Potter grew up in and which, when sitting on Oatmeal Crag high above Esthwaite, imagining 'little tiny fungus people singing and bobbing and dancing' in the leaves and grass at her feet, caused her to muse: 'What heaven can be more real than to retain the spirit-world of childhood, tempered and balanced by knowledge and common–sense . . . yet to feel truly and understand a little, a very little, of the story of life.'

The sisters were born in Salford, near Manchester,

their father holding 'a post in the town offices'. He had come from Flixton in Lancashire, and their mother Mary Anne (nee Whalley) was from Rivington, Lancashire.

William Armitt's health had always been delicate, and his income small. He was therefore anxious to ensure that his daughters' education would enable them to support themselves if necessary. As children they attended the local Islington House Academy, and Annie remembered being taken by a mutual friend to meet Frances Hodgson Burnett who lived in Islington Square and of being introduced as 'fellow authoresses'. Both Annie and the later famous author of *Little Lord Fauntleroy* were then about fourteen years old. Sophia later attended the Manchester School of Art, Annie had literary ambitions, and Louie, who left school at fourteen, began music lessons at Manchester Mechanics Institution School. In 1866 the two eldest sisters spent three months in Paris, where Sophia enjoyed the treasures of the Louvre.

After their father's death when Louie was only fifteen, the sisters decided they would have to set up a school, and moved to a house in Eccles, then becoming a suburb of Manchester. From the beginning with a dozen or so pupils the school thrived, though the sisters felt it prudent to be silent about their ages, and Louie, who was a year younger than their eldest pupil, wore long black clothes in the hope of looking more mature. By 1872 it became necessary to find bigger premises, and with their mother's help from her small portion, two houses, semi-detached, were built to their requirements in Ellesmere Park, one being let, and the other occupied by the school and family.

Though Sophia had been reluctant to give up her formal art studies, she became an outstanding headmistress, and good organiser. They all worked long hours, but travelled extensively in the holidays, at first in Britain but later on the Continent. Their enquiring minds were always active with various researches which they pursued for pleasure in old libraries, museums and art galleries. They also enjoyed Manchester's cultural

10

10. Annie Maria Armitt by Fred Yates.

facilities. Annie was busy reading and learning to write; her first publication appearing in the *Free Lance* when she was seventeen. Sophia and Louie were subscribers to the original Sir Charles Hallé concerts in Manchester. On one occasion in 1877 a piano recital by Rubenstein so moved Louie, who had long aspired to become a good pianist, that on impulse she wrote an article on him, and sent it to the *Manchester City News*. It was immediately published, to her great surprise for she had modestly felt such work was for others. Earlier advice from Ruskin had evidently been taken too much to heart. For when at eighteen she had written to him for guidance, he had replied urging her 'not to wish to write', but to 'exercise yourself in all proper girls' and women's work'! He added: 'Read quietly – history as much as you can – and think – and watch – and be quiet.' Unnecessary words had he but known, for, as with Beatrix Potter, these things were already inherent in her nature. She went on to write future musical critiques, as for example after she had heard the first performance of Mascagni's *Cavalleria Rusticana* at La Scala, Milan. She never achieved her ambition as a pianist, but the musical scholarship reflected in her later publications was of high standing. So much so that a modern musicologist recently expressed surprise that an obscure Victorian lady without special training or the facilities available today could have achieved so much. Sophia and Louie were also members of the Manchester Field Naturalists' Society, some of whose press reports were also written by Louie, while Sophia developed her love of botany and became an expert on wild flowers.

11

11. Louie Armitt by Fred Yates.

In 1877, Annie married her cousin Standford Harris, FRCS of Pendlebury, and two years later, Mrs Armitt died after a long illness. Louie's health was poor, and for some time she and Sophia had longed to retire from their arduous school life. This became possible in 1882 after a legacy from their late uncle Whalley assured an increased income. Their school was sold, and they left Eccles. For the next four years they spent the winters with their aunt

12

12. Louie Armitt in an Oxford Garden, painted by Sophia.

Whalley at Bowden in Cheshire, and their summers abroad.

During this period they also spent some winter months in Oxford, where Louie researched old unpublished manuscripts in the Duke Humphrey's part of the Bodleian Library. This work, together with studies made in the Royal Library in Brussels on a sixteenth-century work published in Venice, bore fruit in the articles mentioned above. They appeared mainly in the *Musical Times* and the *Musical News* magazines in the 1890s. Meanwhile Sophia had also been busy. She produced some fine drawings of Oxford's colleges and famous buildings together with watercolours like that of the interior of the Bodleian. This is an interesting record of the 1880s, and similar in technique to Beatrix Potter's 1882 watercolour of Wray Castle Library (see page 27).

13

In 1886, Annie's husband had retired from medical practice in poor health, and the couple had leased Esthwaite Mount, at Colthouse near Hawkshead in the Lake District. Louie was still unwell with heart trouble, and she and Sophia decided to live at Hawkshead too. They found rooms at Borwick Lodge where they happily spent the next eight years. The house stood on the fell-side with lovely mountain views to the north, and a fine view over Esthwaite Water to the south. A carriage was available for hire as required, and here they settled without the burden of domestic cares to enjoy their books, writing, gardening, sketching, embroidery and wood-carving, a Ruskin-inspired craft started locally by their friend Hardwicke Rawnsley. The sisters helped village activities and attended Hawkshead Church, soon becoming intimate with the local families. Sophia joined

13. The Bodleian Library, Oxford, by Sophia Armitt, 1887.

14. High Street, Oxford, by Sophia, 1885.

14

15

a botanical society, and for the rest of her life wrote monthly articles for its magazine. On one occasion she also dined at Brantwood and met Ruskin, who spoke kindly of her art work, and gave her permission to copy pictures in his collection.

In 1894 Borwick Lodge was no longer available, and Esthwaite Mount had been given up. Their brother-in-law went abroad to receive special nursing, and was only to live a few years longer. Sophia and Louie put their goods in store and spent the winter in Manchester and Cambridge, while Annie, who was not well, sought treatment in Newcastle. They wanted to return to the Lake Country, and eventually settled in 1896 in their final home: Rydal Cottage on the banks of the Rothay, where Annie temporarily joined them until strong enough to move into nearby Rothay Lodge.

At Rydal they found themselves part of an intellectual milieu. Frances Arnold of Fox How became a close friend,

15. The interior of Hawkshead Church by Sophia Armitt, 1887.

16. Borwick Lodge, the sisters' home from 1886 to 1894, painted by Sophia in 1887.

17

17. Rydal Cottage, a design from Annie Maria's bookplate, 1912.

18. Charlotte Mason by Fred Yates.

18

and could tell them at first hand of Wordsworth, Harriet Martineau, and, with her late brother Matthew Arnold, of meeting Charlotte Brontë at Fox How. The sisters met her distinguished visitors, and it became customary after Sunday service for her guests to call at Rydal Cottage to admire Sophia's beautiful garden by the river.

They had long been aware of educational pioneers and the continuing struggle for women to have the right to graduate from the universities of Oxford and Cambridge. But at Rydal, through their friendship with Charlotte Mason, they actually met pioneers like Dorothea Beale, and Miss Mason could tell them of others she had known like Anne Jemima Clough, Frances M. Buss, and Emily Davies. No doubt this is why Sophia started local Oxford Extension Lectures, and became secretary of the Technical Classes. Charlotte Mason had established the Parents' National Educational Union, and the House of Education in Rydal Road, Ambleside in 1892, and the sisters, like the Rawnsleys, became part of 'her little coterie' of neighbours invited to her weekly drawing-room evenings. An individual chosen in advance would read a paper, usually on a poetic or literary subject, and these papers were sometimes published in the *Parents' Review*, which she edited.

Charlotte Mason had earlier lectured throughout the country, as well as corresponding for years with most of the leading educationalists, and so had become well known. But just how well known is perhaps best illustrated by the surprising visit in 1895 to her House of Education at Scale How, Ambleside, of Madam Shimoda from Japan. At a time when Japan tended to regard Britain with suspicion, this delightful aristocratic lady had not only been sent by the Japanese emperor to study methods of education in Europe and America, but had

Charlotte Mason's establishment on her itinerary. A document recently received by the Armitt Trust from the archives of the Imperial Household of Japan shows that Madam Shimoda was in London in 1894, and under the patronage of the Duchess of Portland had been welcomed into London society. She was even presented to Queen Victoria, and her visit reported in *The Times*. She then stayed some time in Ambleside, and instructed the students in brush drawing and paper cutting and folding. According to Miss Kitching of Scale How, she was a court poetess and belonged to the emperor's private circle. In the evenings she wore court dress, a beautiful kimono of special design with the emperor's private signet, and her dainty appearance was much admired. Eventually she returned to the Imperial Household to start a school for 'peeresses'.

At Rydal Louie also met and corresponded with J.R. Magrath, Provost of Queen's College, Oxford, the don who, unusually for those days, wholeheartedly approved

19. Frances Arnold of Fox How.

20. A landscape of Rydal Water painted by J. Bourne in the 1790s.

21. Pen-and-wash drawing by Sophia Armitt of Pillar House, Hawkshead, 1886.

21

of higher education for women, and who had been a chief supporter of Dorothea Beale's work at Cheltenham and Oxford. When Louie's heart trouble prevented her travelling to reference libraries, she had taken up local history studies because Rydal Hall contained important muniments which the squire Mr Fleming had kindly made available. J. R. Magrath was also using them in his current editing of *The Flemings at Oxford*, and in the preface he acknowledged the help she was able to give. She also joined the London Library for the same reason and received books by post.

The sisters became loved and respected figures, writing, teaching and lecturing. They had a busy correspondence with experts in various fields, particularly natural history, and enjoyed the company of local artists and writers. Annie lived on in poor health until 1933, but Sophia died in 1908, followed by Louie in 1911. Canon Rawnsley's sonnet, written for the formal opening of the Armitt Library, paid just tribute to the sisters 'who sowed that other minds might reap'.

BEATRIX POTTER AND THE ARMITT LIBRARY

It has gradually become evident that Beatrix Potter lived her life in separate compartments, and this was certainly the case with her Armitt membership. Apart from her husband William, the Hawkshead solicitor who became an early member and trustee, even her family seemed unaware of her connection.

Quiet and secretive by nature, she had in her youth committed her inmost thoughts to her private journal in a self-invented code. Later too, she saw little need to chatter about her personal affairs, or even to correct any misconceptions, as her often reported encounter with the tramp at Sawrey confirms. Because during her farming years she wore clogs, and a sack fastened with a safety-pin round her shoulders in the rain, she quietly enjoyed the joke when the said tramp commiserated with her, mistaking the prosperous author of *The Tale of Peter Rabbit*, for one of his own fraternity. Similarly, when she went up to London for her wedding in 1913, not until her return did she trouble to inform her astonished house-keeper Mrs Rogerson that her mistress Miss Potter had become Mrs W. H. Heelis. Such examples are many.

22. Beatrix Potter, photographed by her father Rupert in October 1882.

If Beatrix's secrecy has denied posterity knowledge of her personal encounters with Armitt Library affairs, there is a great deal of circumstantial evidence with which to reconstruct her interest in the trust and approval of the sisters' aims and ideals. They were all kindred spirits. Years before the library was founded, she clearly knew all about the sisters, and particularly of Sophia's botanical work and Louie's various natural history studies. And yet, surprisingly, we don't know how or when they first met, and no letters have survived.

The fortunes of these four young ladies, however, were far apart. Beatrix had been born in South Kensington, London, in 1866 of parents with inherited wealth from Lancashire cotton fortunes. Her father Rupert, educated in Manchester, later took his Bar Finals in London. Though called to the Bar, he never practised, but lived a life of independent means between his Bolton Gardens home near the then new Natural History Musuem and his London clubs, the Athenaeum and the Reform. He took his family on regular holidays, usually to the seaside in spring, and the country in summer when he leased large houses: at first in Scotland, and later in the Lake District. Apart from occasional family visits, Beatrix and her young brother Bertram lived restricted lives. She was never sent to school or allowed companions because her mother felt her health was delicate. Like the Armitt sisters she read and studied intensively, and enjoyed visiting museums and art galleries, but, at the age of nineteen, after a visit to the theatre by carriage she confessed: 'Extraordinary to state, it was the first time in my life that I have been past the Horse Guards, Admiralty, or seen the Strand and the Monument.'

23. Beatrix with her father Rupert and brother Bertram at Lingholm, Keswick, in 1885.

23

Hardwicke Rawnsley, a mutual friend of both Beatrix and the Armitt sisters, almost certainly acted as a catalyst in stimulating their thoughts in similar directions and reporting each other's interests and current work. His long-lasting friendship with the Potter family had begun in 1882 when he was vicar of St Margaret's Church, Low Wray, near the north-west shore of Windermere and Beatrix's father leased Wray Castle on Windermere for the summer. In 1883 Hardwicke Rawnsley became the incumbent of Crosthwaite Church near Keswick. He and his wife Edith renewed acquaintance with the Potters when they spent the summer months at Lingholm near Keswick in 1885, and the friendship continued with subsequent visits.

The Armitt sisters had also spent many holidays in the Lake District long before they lived there permanently. Indeed, their mother had once taken Rydal Cottage for a family holiday twenty-one years before it became the sisters' final home in 1896. Hardwicke Rawnsley was well known to them; he had become a public figure, and Annie, for example, had been a guest at Wray Vicarage

24. Derwentwater by moonlight, painted by J. Bourne in the 1790s.

25. A painting of the library at Wray Castle made by Beatrix during her visit there in 1882.

before she went to live in the Hawkshead valley. He may have told them of Beatrix Potter soon after his meeting with her family in 1882 or on one of the sisters' holidays in Keswick when he was vicar of Crosthwaite Church.

Beatrix would have felt an affinity with the sisters' Manchester cultural background. Her grandfather, Liberal MP for Carlisle, and a friend of Cobden and Bright, had been President of the Manchester School of Art where Sophia had studied. They all knew places like Owen's College Museum where Beatrix had enjoyed viewing the fossil collection, near the site of her father's birthplace and the later Manchester University. The whole area was steeped in the family history and associations of both her parents, and she enjoyed exploring their old haunts. She had even visited Eccles in 1884, where she admired the fine old market cross.

Louie Armitt was very similar in temperament to Beatrix, but was fifteen years her senior, the same age as Hardwicke Rawnsley. Like Beatrix she was reserved and shy, and once chided herself in her diary for allowing the servants to bully her. She too however, had very positive ideas, and great determination to achieve something worthwhile. Louie, also like Beatrix, kept a secret diary from the age of fifteen, and sometimes the comments of

26. Sophia's drawing of her sister Louie as a young woman.

26

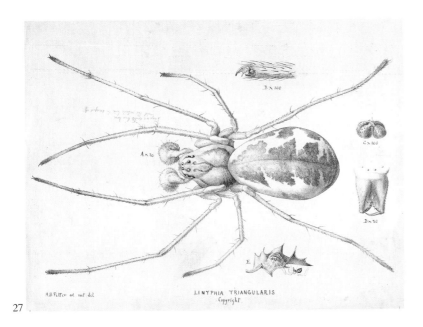

27.

27. Microscope study of a
Sheet Web Spider by Beatrix
ca. 1895.

these two young Victorian ladies show an almost
startling accord. Visiting Westminster Abbey aged
twenty-four on Easter Sunday when Dean Stanley (Dr
Arnold's well-known biographer) was preaching,
Louie's entry records: '"I know that my Redeemer
liveth" was sung while the golden sunlight fell through
the high windows in bright patches upon the richly
carved walls above, and never lightened the gloom
below. I shall never forget.' Years later, Beatrix then in
her late twenties, wrote: 'Went to Westminster Abbey
too late to see round, but heard part of the Service and the
Anthem: most wonderful and beautiful looking up into
the shadowy vaulted roof. I shall not soon forget my
thoughts.' Their opinions of pictures in contemporary
London exhibitions were also often similar, especially
those of the Pre-Raphaelites.

It is surely more than coincidence that these ladies were
often working on similar natural history themes. In 1905
Louie wrote an excellent paper in *The Naturalist* on 'Some
Observations on Spiders at Rydal' which contained
information about the Sheet Web Spider (*Linyphia
triangularis*), a subject on which Beatrix had prepared a
microscope study for a lithograph in about 1895. Written

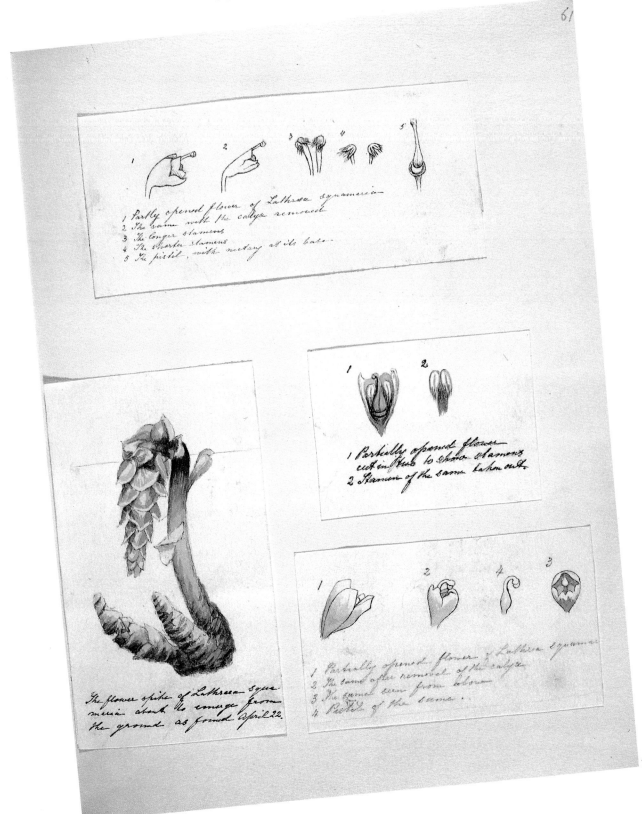

1 Partly opened flower of *Lathraea squamaria*
2 The same with the calyx removed
3 The longer stamens
4 The shorter stamens
5 The pistil, with nectary at its base.

1 Partially opened flower
cut in two to show stamens
2 Stamen of the same taken out

The flower spike of *Lathraea squamaria* about to emerge from
the ground as found April 22.

1 Partially opened flower of *Lathraea squamaria*
2 The same after removal of the calyx
3 The same seen from above
4 Pistil of the same.

29

Cantharellus cibarius.
sent by N.G. from Bala N. Wales
august 20. 07

in Louie's pleasing but simple prose, with great clarity of thought, the reader enters a mysterious world of quiet contemplation which is almost poetic, though in no way sentimental. And from the 1890s Sophia was painting specimens of Rydal fungi in watercolours. These drawings though competent and pleasing do not have the exceptional quality of those studies by Beatrix which combined scientific accuracy of colour, scale and form, with an almost ethereal quality. Sophia's best artistic skills lay more in her pen and wash architectural drawings of cathedrals and old buildings (see pages 19, 24). What is of particular interest, though, is that, as in the case of Beatrix's earliest fungus drawings, Sophia's studies did not at first include detailed sections of the stem as suggested to Beatrix by Charles McIntosh, the Scottish mycologist. In a letter to Miss Potter in 1894 this amateur naturalist had written: ' . . . you can make them more perfect as botanical drawings, by making separate sketches showing the attachments of the gills, the stem if it be hollow or otherwise, or any other detail that will

28, 29. Pages from Sophia Armitt's botanical notebooks.

show the characteristics of the plant more distinctly.' From that time sections were always produced, and this was also the case with Sophia's subsequent fungi studies. It seems possible, therefore, that Beatrix actually discussed Charles McIntosh's letter with Sophia.

Beatrix later gave this significant letter to the Armitt Library, together with her copy of *A Perthshire Naturalist* (Coates, 1923), the posthumous biography of McIntosh. Another example of work on the same themes occurred when Louie wrote an article in about 1894 for young people on the mysteries of the symbiotic nature of lichen, using it as a parable of the need to work together. This scientific subject was of deep interest to Beatrix in her 1896 microscope work and experiments.

From her retirement Sophia was particularly active with her botanical studies and drawings. Apart from her monthly botanical articles and contributions in Charlotte Mason's *Parents' Review* magazines, she had some articles published in *Science Gossip*, the prestigious London publication for the exchange of information for scientists and lovers of nature. She was also busy adding to her extensive collection of pressed botanical specimens, including many flowers from abroad. She loved travelling, especially to Alpine meadows and art galleries, and continued to go abroad even after 1899 when heart trouble marked the end of Louie's continental journeys.

Sophia's researches necessitated some visits to the Royal Botanic Gardens, Kew, and it is intriguing to compare her experiences with those of Beatrix, recounted by Dr Noble later in this book. In spite of being escorted by her uncle Sir Henry Roscoe, FRS, the distinguished chemist, Beatrix found Kew officialdom unhelpful and dispiriting. Similarly, her experiences at the Natural History Museum were often exasperating. 'I worked into indignation about that august Institution,' she wrote in 1896. 'They have reached such a pitch of propriety that one cannot ask the simplest question.' She added: 'The clerks seem to be all gentlemen and one must

30. Examples of Sophia Armitt's botanical drawings.

31–35 (over page). Some of Beatrix Potter's studies of fungi from Scotland.

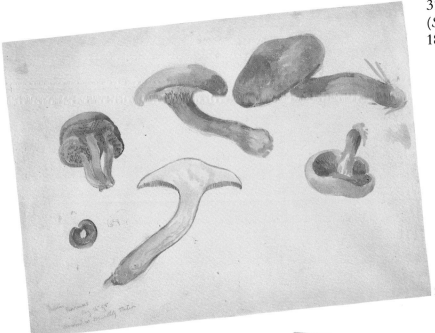

31. Brown Cow Bolete (*Suillus bovinus*), August 1895.

32. Chanterelle (*Cantharellus cibarius*), August 1895.

33. Clouded Agaric (*Clitocybe nebularis*), November 1893.

34. *Russula lepida*, August 1894.

34

35. *Pholiota* species, September 1893.

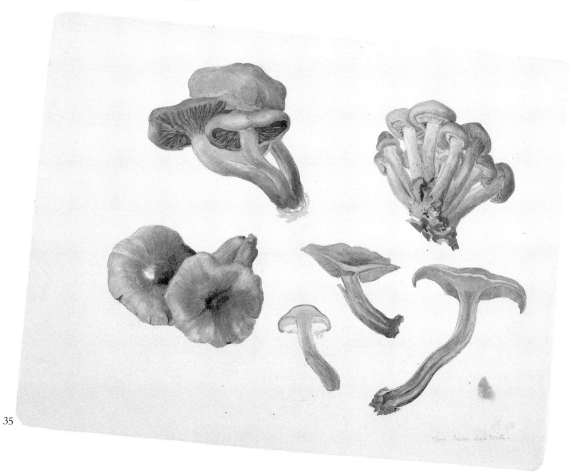

35

not speak to them. If people are forward I can manage them, but if they take the line of being shocked it is perfectly awful to a shy person.' Sophia visited Kew several times, and on 8 May 1884, Louie's diary recorded: 'Went with Sophia alone to Kew where she penetrated the herbarium with a few Tyrolean plants [dried specimens] that she was unable to name. At first, it seemed from the constitution of the place no help could be given her, but Professor Oliver [Keeper of the Herbarium] seemed loth to let her go, and at last took her up into the library, and provided her with some botanical works which were of considerable assistance.'

Perhaps what Annie Maria had once called her sister Sophia's 'naturally masterful and imperious manner' had helped on this occasion, but she was probably not aware how privileged she was. The time was just not propitious for amateur scientists like Beatrix and Sophia to get the help and facilities they required from national museums and institutions. The system was then very rigid and designed for experts only. Readers' tickets were rarely issued for amateurs, so that for an ordinary member of the public like Sophia not only to have 'penetrated the herbarium' but also to have gained entry to the library was decidedly unusual.

36. The Royal Botanic Gardens at Kew in the 1890s.

36

LATER YEARS

Sophia and Louie had died before their library was opened, but Beatrix's involvement with Armitt affairs continued for another thirty years.

From the turn of the new century, various circumstances had changed the course of Beatrix's creative activities. The discouragement of her scientific studies by unsympathetic officials coincided with the opening up of new possibilities. Having reached her mid-thirties, she had increasingly longed for some financial independence, and found to her delight that her animal drawings were saleable for book illustrations. This led to her creation of *The Tale of Peter Rabbit*, and when the book was refused by at least six publishers, she decided to publish it herself. It was successful, and the following year, 1902, Messrs Frederick Warne and Co. agreed to publish it commercially, and subsequently the whole series of twenty-three titles that followed.

In 1905 with her regular royalty cheques and with the additional help of a small legacy she bought Hill Top Farm in her favourite Lakeland village of Near Sawrey, followed by the purchase of the nearby Castle Cottage Farm in 1909.

Sawrey is in the parish of Claife, and from 1905 Beatrix automatically became one of the *Landowners of Claife*, a body set up after the Claife Heights Commons Enclosure Award of 1799 to protect freeholders' rights granted under that award. They consisted mainly of rights to take gravel from Esthwaite and Windermere lake sites, and stone from small quarries for the repair and maintenance of private roads and property. Over the years the committee also dealt with practical matters like safeguarding old boundaries, and regulating the felling of dangerous timber. Inevitably, however, confusion sometimes arose as to the exact legal demarcation of freeholders' rights and parish council responsibilities. Beatrix took a lively interest in all this and as early as 1912, when still mainly resident in London, she was

37

38

elected to the Landowners' committee as a
Representative Freeholder.

Becoming a property owner had brought her into close
contact with the local solicitor William Heelis, and in
1913 they married. She happily settled down to savour
country life with William, and, though still a dutiful
Victorian daughter busy with her parents' needs, she
enjoyed her new-found freedom at Castle Cottage. Over
the next few years her creative work as artist and writer
gradually gave way to farming interests; especially the
breeding of Herdwick sheep.

Village life also brought her into closer contact with
earlier acquaintances she had shared with the Armitt
sisters; people like Mrs Alcock Beck of Esthwaite Lodge
on the western shore of Esthwaite. Beatrix's journal

38. Beatrix and William
Heelis on their wedding day.

37. Hill Top by night, a
watercolour by Beatrix
dating from about 1910.

recorded meeting her in 1896 when she, Beatrix, was buying 'two striped petticoats' in Hawkshead. She described Mrs Beck as a 'pleasant, friendly, middle-aged lady', a fitting description of this kindly soul who was always active in village welfare. Thomas Alcock Beck, her husband's forebear who built the house, was the historian and mediaeval scholar who wrote *Annales Furnesienses* in 1844, the history of Furness Abbey dedicated to Queen Victoria. Today the Armitt Library houses this painstaking work together with documents and botanical records of the author's garden.

The mutual friend who had been closest to the Armitt sisters and Beatrix was Emily Jane Fowkes, a member of the Satterthwaite family, Quakers connected with Colthouse for centuries. Even after the Armitt sisters had moved to Rydal, their friendship with Emily Jane flourished by letter and reciprocal visits. In 1887 she had married Frederick Fowkes, the pioneer electrical engineer whose feat of cooking cutlets with 'the electric light' Beatrix had noted in 1896. They lived at Waterside, Claife, between Colthouse and Sawrey, where Frederick Fowkes generated his own electricity powered by tarns he had built on family land on Claife Heights. His early electric car was also a local wonder.

In later years Beatrix sometimes attended the Colthouse Quaker Meeting House with Mrs Fowkes who contributed to some of Beatrix's favourite good causes; especially the Invalid Children's Aid Association, and the Hawkshead and District Nursing Association, founded mainly by

39. Emily Jane Fowkes.

39

her and endowed with a cottage so that Hawkshead could have a resident district nurse. Beatrix knew Mr Fowkes well for he was the secretary of the Landowners' committee on which her shrewd common sense proved a welcome asset. His son, Michael Satterthwaite Fowkes, always called 'Jack', sometimes went fishing with Willie Heelis, and on one occasion he took his own small and rather shy son Dick to call as arranged at Castle Cottage *en route* to Moss Eccles Tarn. Dick vividly remembers Mrs Heelis suddenly appearing in clogs and rough old clothes and speaking to him so sharply that he was very relieved when Mr Heelis appeared, rod in hand. Beatrix was always kind to the family, though, and gave signed copies of her books to Emily Jane's children and grandchildren, and on one special occasion gave one of her hand-made Peter Rabbit dolls which the family still treasures.

During her farming years at Hill Top, Beatrix always took a sympathetic interest in both the Girl Guides and Boy Scouts, and allowed them to camp on her land. (She would of course have been aware that Baden-Powell himself acknowledged that it was Charlotte Mason's work with young people which had inspired him to found the Scout movement.) In the 1930s she invited Bruce Logan Thompson of Troutbeck to bring his troop to camp on her land there, and the boys remember her as being 'the soul of kindness'. Bruce Thompson was the Armitt official who knew her best for over a quarter of a century. He was a member of a local family at one time proprietors of The Low Wood and Ferry House Inns, hotels known to the Potter family. He had joined the Armitt Library in 1924, and served the trust for over 50 years, becoming a trustee, Hon. Librarian, and later Chairman. At the time of the Troutbeck camp, Bruce was secretary at the London offices of the National Trust, and also the Scoutmaster of the Kensington Troop, which included many poor boys whom Beatrix wished to enjoy a country holiday.

Bruce Thompson was also appointed in 1936 as

41. Beatrix Potter at the Woolpack Show, Eskdale, in 1931.

National Trust Agent for the North, and it was in this capacity that he came into closest contact with Mrs Heelis. Some time earlier the National Trust had asked her if she would temporarily manage the Monk Coniston Estate, pending the appointment of a land agent, and this was agreed. The shrewd and elderly lady with practical experience did not always see eye to eye with the quiet young man, but though she was always quick to criticise if she thought it necessary, they came to understand each other. Indeed, it was because of loyalty to her that his extensive knowledge of her and her Armitt associations, mostly died with him. Knowing of her wish for privacy, when asked about her he always quietly demurred, saying that she disliked publicity. He wrote *The Lake District & The National Trust* (1946), a well-received book of which Beatrix would surely have approved. Full of interest, it reflects his commitment to the principles laid down by the idealistic Canon Rawnsley, and records Beatrix Potter's exceptional benefactions to the National Trust.

40. View across Esthwaite Water today, photographed by Cressida Pemberton-Pigott.

40

BEATRIX POTTER – ARMITT BENEFACTOR

Beatrix's gifts to the Armitt Library began in 1933 when she gave 122 volumes from the library of her late father. They consisted mainly of works on art, history, biography, literature and natural history. As was customary, a small neat label was designed for the inside book covers to record the gifts, and Beatrix thought it 'very nice' with the proviso that 'Mrs.' and 'Esq.' should be omitted, viz: 'This book with many others was presented to the Armitt Library by Beatrix Heelis from the library of her father the late Rupert Potter.' Most of the books also contained her father's book-plate.

42. Herbert Bell by Fred Yates.

42

Writing to Herbert Bell, Hon. Armitt Librarian, on 30 March 1933, she regretted that other books had earlier been sent to auction: 'They made about £15, which was as much as could be expected; I think the booksellers form a ring, and unless there were outside bidders – they had their own way.' She added: 'I have a nice collection of books of my own but perhaps not quite such standard books of reference as my father's. When my time comes I should be very glad if some more were found suitable for the Armitt Library – I fancy a good many of mine would be duplicate [*sic*] with works already on your shelves, certainly one could not hope to have any local topography worth offering – your collection is wonderfully complete.' She was referring to the outstanding nature of the library's collection of Lake District topography, given mainly by one of its most important benefactors, Alderman Plummer, a Manchester bibliophile, Chairman of Libraries there, and Governor of the famous John Rylands Library which now holds the papers of Beatrix's uncle Sir Henry Roscoe.

Wordsworth's grandson, Gordon G. Wordsworth, still active on the Armitt Library Committee, sent a personal letter of thanks to which Beatrix replied: 'I am glad that the volumes have found a peaceful home. It is very unpleasant to have to auction family possessions, and I have the feeling that my father would have been

43. Dr Syntax and the Bookseller, a plate from one of Rupert Potter's books donated to the Armitt Library by Beatrix.

vexed to see books that *he* valued selling for next to nothing. I kept a good many.' On the quandary of reconciling the need for security with accessibility for use, she commented: 'The Armitt Library does seem rather solitary. But these books are not of a rarity to appeal to burglars (provided you and Mr Bell don't say too much in their praise!) and Tom, Dick and friends are more likely to patronize the public library where there are novels; or to scratch their tiresome names in the open air. It would be a pity if they were disfigured; but I hardly think it likely.' She imagined 'the worst risk . . . would be if there were ever a local bibliomaniac afflicted with kleptomania'. Her letter ended: 'I have found a long (and very dull) letter of W.W.'s [William Wordsworth] – I will leave it with Mr Bell sometime – It appears genuine.'

Five years later she donated a further twelve volumes, some of which may have come from a local book sale, for three months earlier she had written again to Herbert Bell: 'I made a note of some books at Tower Bank – there are very few, nearly everything was sold after Mrs Alcock Beck died. I should be very glad to send the car for you on Thursday afternoon . . . That would give you time to look at the little collection at Tower Bank – then I will come there and show you A.J.H.'s books at Hill Top – and we will get you home after a cup of tea.' (A.J.H. was William Heelis's late brother, Arthur.)

She gave the largest number of books in September 1941, two years before her death, and over the years a few sundry items had also been given: things like agricultural show catalogues, leaflets, a little sheepdog sketch on a scrap of notepaper, and an amusing invoice from a local farmer with the message, 'To Mrs. Heelis, Your pigs are ready but there is no girl pigs.' Evidently the poor man had taxed his brain as to how a Victorian lady should be addressed on so delicate a matter! An undated letter from her 'affec. nephew J.H. Leech' in the Isle of Wight, another budding naturalist, was tucked into Vol. I of the greatly treasured set of Morris' *British Moths* which Beatrix had presented. Addressing Beatrix as 'Dear Aunt Helen', it recorded the despatch of 'some caterpillars of the 3 spot burnet "Lonicera Trifolii" [*sic*] the real food plant is trefoil but I think you will find that they eat clover and vetch', and ends with the hope they will 'turn out well'.

After Beatrix died on 22 December 1943, Warne generously presented a set of first editions of her little masterpieces from the Peter Rabbit series, together with a *Peter Rabbit's Almanac for 1929*. Similarly, the American publisher, the Horn Book Inc., of Boston, gave a copy of her *Wag-by-Wall*, published posthumously by them in 1944. Beatrix had also bequeathed a final forty-three books, received in 1946, and these included her two privately printed works, *The Tale of Peter Rabbit* and *The Tailor of Gloucester*, and first editions of *The Fairy Caravan* and *Sister Anne*. Various other material has been received in more recent years.

All these gifts are greatly prized, but above all, the thing which makes this Beatrix Potter collection outstanding is her generous gift of hundreds of watercolour studies, which include some of her finest work. They comprise large numbers of paintings of fungi, mosses, lichens, archaeological artefacts, and sundry items like a pine cone and fossils from Troutbeck. All the mycological paintings were originally stored in eight portfolios made by Beatrix herself from boards covered in patterned cottons (perhaps samples from her grandfather's calico printing works) and lined with plain cotton. In addition, she gave a similar portfolio of her important microscope drawings intelligible only to the expert. Two other folios, one in white vellum, contained her archaeological paintings and sundry items. The first paintings received were her studies of Roman artefacts from London given in 1935, together with two sketch maps and notes on their provenance.

Beatrix kept the fungus studies at home for her own reference, and sometimes showed them to special visitors. After her death they were given to the Armitt Library 'in compliance with her expressed wish'. Her husband, still serving on the Armitt committee, was present when the gift was formally acknowledged.

44

44. One of Beatrix's fabric portfolios.

45

45. The Armitt Library today, temporarily housed in Kelsick Road, Ambleside. Photograph by Cressida Pemberton-Pigott.

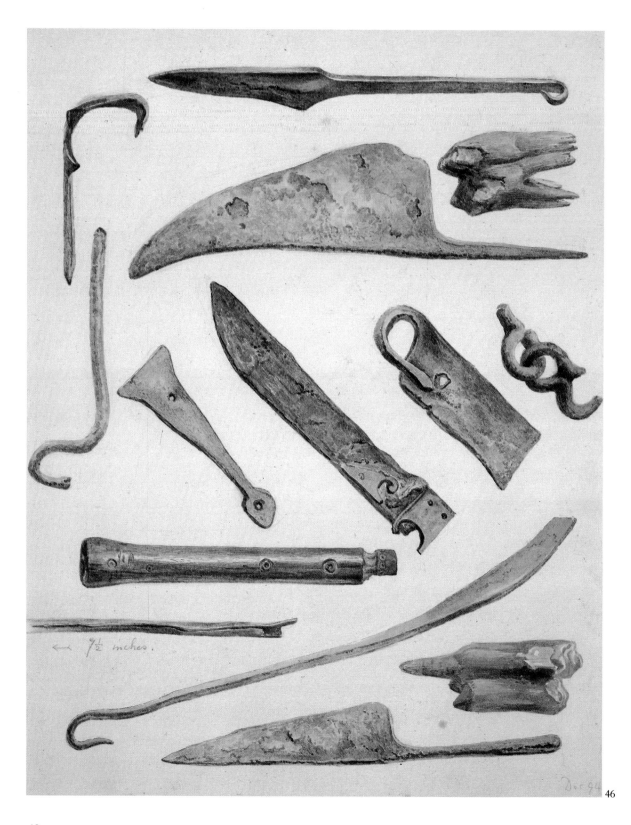

← 7½ inches.

46

BEATRIX POTTER'S
ARCHAEOLOGY
by Eileen Jay

In 1933 Beatrix Potter wrote to Herbert Bell about the Armitt Collection, 'When I am less busy I would like to have a good look at the Roman remains and I will bring some watercolour drawings to show you – of some very fine sandals out of Fleet ditch.'[1]

It had been Louie Armitt's wish that the library might include a small museum 'that should illustrate the life of Ambleside through the long past to the present'. Gradually, items of local interest were presented, consisting mainly of prehistoric artefacts found in the Grasmere, Langdale, Ambleside and Windermere areas, local Roman finds, and sundry items from later times.

The story of the Roman collection goes back to the earliest days of the trust when members were active in conservation projects. Willingham Franklin Rawnsley, trustee and early Chairman, discovered that Borrans Field, the beautiful twenty-acre site of the Roman fort Galava on Windermere's north-east shore, first described by Camden centuries before, was in imminent danger of being covered with boarding houses. So he started an appeal fund, run by members like Gordon Wordsworth and Herbert Bell. In an undated letter to Annie Maria Armitt he wrote: 'I feel no doubt that we shall save it [Borrans Field] and am proud to think that *I* set the question going when it seemed already a Lost cause. I went with Gordon Wordsworth and Hugh Redmayne to beard the builder in his den and got him to stop digging his foundations till we could get the needful purchase money.' His confidence was justified. The necessary £4,000 was raised by public subscription in 1912 and the site bought for the National Trust.

---

[1] In Beatrix's original account of the drawings she gave the provenance as the Walbrook.

47

47. Drawings of potsherds.

46. A sheet of Beatrix Potter's London archaeological drawings, 1894: metal and bone objects from the Bucklersbury excavations.

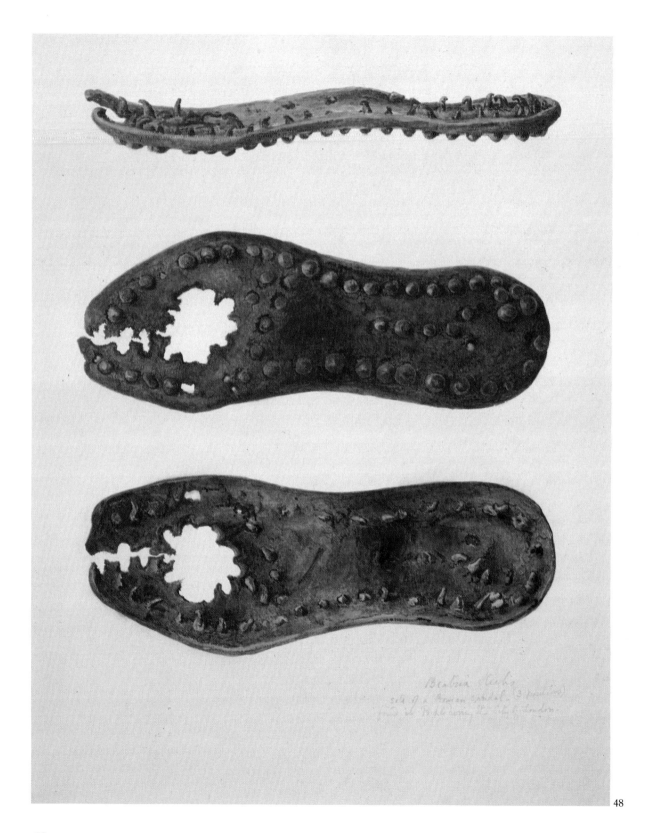

The Armitt Trust was fortunate in having the voluntary services of the internationally admired philosopher, historian and archaeologist, Robin G. Collingwood. His father, W.G. Collingwood, artist, historian, and friend and secretary of Ruskin, had been the exacting editor of Louie Armitt's local history papers. (Both Collingwoods were Armitt members, as was the father's protégé Arthur Ransome.) Robin Collingwood, born in the Lake District at Cartmel Fell in 1889 and later of Coniston and Oxford, was once described as one of

49

48, 50. Roman shoe leathers from the London excavations.

49. Robin Collingwood.

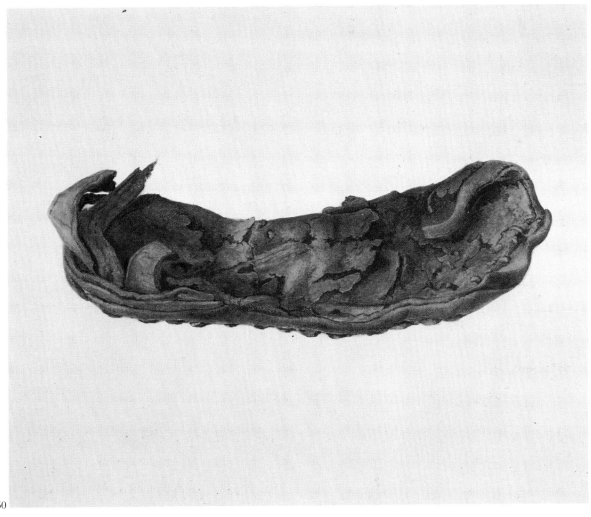

50

52. Needles and toilet utensils from the Roman site, City of London.

51. Beatrix's drawings of Roman shoe leather sandal fragments, 1895.

the most learned men of his generation. He spent four years (1913–15 and 1920) excavating the Ambleside fort, working with Professor Haverfield in the first year. The project was disrupted by the First World War when he served in the Intelligence Department of the Admiralty.

For several years in the 1920s the Roman finds languished in the hut on site because of practical problems in housing. Then in 1929, through the negotiations of Robin Collingwood, the collection was given to the Armitt Trust, then housed in an Ambleside cottage. In the early thirties the Armitt Library acquired the larger premises known as the Orchard through the generosity of Herbert Bell's father, who donated, with certain provisos, the remainder of his long lease to the trust. Robin advised the trustees how to prepare the new Museum Room there and, helped by his wife, arranged to professional standards the display of Roman artefacts found on the Borrans Field site. He also supplied a model

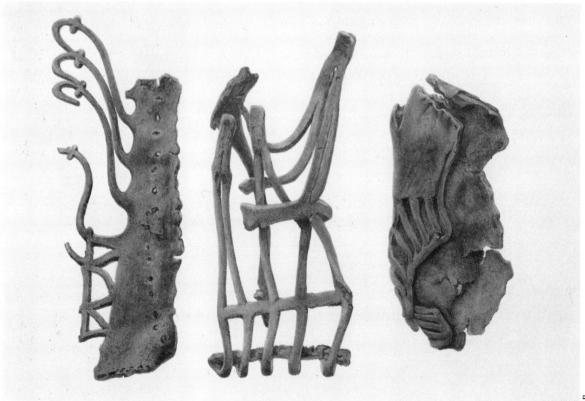

51

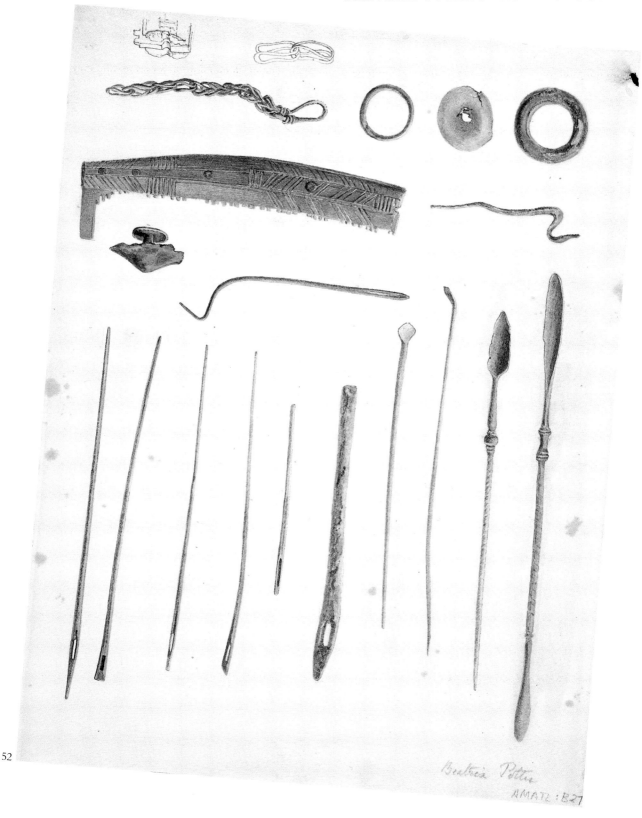

52

53

53, 54. Pieces of Roman pottery from the City of London site. 54 shows Samian ware.

of the fort. For many years until the lease expired the Museum Room was maintained by the trust as a public amenity.

Beatrix was of course fully aware of the part played by the Armitt Trust in the Borrans Field story. When, following her letter to Herbert Bell, she did 'have a good look at the Roman remains' from the Ambleside fort, she liked the display and her gift of archaeological watercolours followed. These drawings of the 1890s form an archaeological record of everyday Roman and post-Roman objects which had been found in London in the silts of the Walbrook stream, and from the historic settlements of Southwark. A family friend had lent Beatrix the artefacts to draw, just when she was at the height of her powers as a scientific illustrator. The watercolours, all carefully drawn to scale, are unusual in combining professional accuracy with that aesthetic quality so characteristic of her work. They also form a unique addition to the official London records for, in the rather casual Victorian tradition of archaeological enquiry, the original artefacts were given to a private individual and have since disappeared.

For the next forty years or so Beatrix Potter's beautiful archaeological paintings could be viewed at the Armitt Museum, until the lease of the Orchard finally expired.

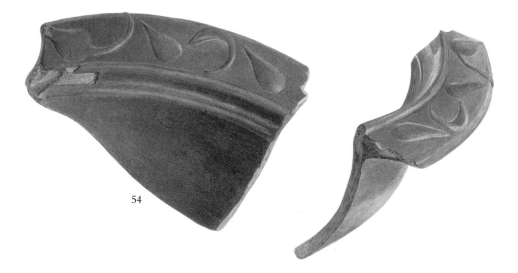

BEATRIX POTTER AND CHARLES McINTOSH, NATURALISTS
by Mary Noble

PERSONAL PREFACE

About fifteen years ago I was researching the history of mycology (the study of fungi) in Scotland and was particularly interested in the life and works of Charles McIntosh (1839–1922), known as the Perthshire Naturalist, who lived at Inver, near Dunkeld in Perthshire. When he died, a book to commemorate him was compiled by Henry Coates.[1] After publication the relevant papers were returned to Charles McIntosh's niece, Miss E.M.MacIntosh, then living in Dunkeld, who kept the parcel unopened for fifty years until I asked her for more information about her uncle. She gave it to me to look through, as 'there might be something to help you'. I found many extremely interesting papers, including letters from botanical authorities of the time, but I was astonished to find also letters from the Potter family, three from Mr Rupert Potter and twelve from his daughter Beatrix. These were all about what she called 'funguses', lichens and even mosses. These documents are referred to from now on as the Dunkeld Letters.

At that time I knew very little about Beatrix Potter except that she had written splendid books for children and had made some fine watercolour paintings of fungi which were reproduced in *Wayside and Woodland Fungi* by Dr W. P. K. Findlay (1967). Any study in depth of these paintings was not possible, however, because of difficulties pertaining to their conservation.

Exhibitions of Beatrix's paintings of fungi had been held in various sites in Britain – Kendal, Ambleside,

---

[1] *A Perthshire Naturalist: Charles Macintosh of Inver* by Henry Coates, T. Fisher Unwin Ltd, 1923.

Perth, Edinburgh – and abroad in America, Canada and Australia but always these selected originals had to be kept in subdued light. In 1954 a special selection was shown to the members of the British Mycological Society at Windermere in the Lake District. Dr F. B. Hora, a past president, wrote in reporting this meeting, 'A most memorable experience was the exhibition of paintings of toadstools made by the late Miss Beatrix Potter, well known as the author and illustrator of many popular children's books. For myself, they are, of their kind, the best I have seen, not a detail has been missed.' Another member of the British Mycological Society appreciated the scientific accuracy of the paintings as well as their beauty; this was the late Dr W. P. K. Findlay, who selected about sixty to illustrate *Wayside and Woodland Fungi*.

My early training in mycology did not include 'toadstools' but with the most generous support of the experts at the Royal Botanic Garden, Edinburgh, especially Dr Roy Watling, I began to do work on Beatrix Potter's mycology as revealed in the Dunkeld Letters. It was with considerable pleasure that in 1981 I was able to give a paper before my fellow mycologists at a meeting of the British Mycological Society held in the Royal Botanic Gardens, Kew. Dr Findlay was present and heard for the first time about the influence of Charles McIntosh on Beatrix's mycology and he encouraged me to continue this study. In the next year I had the privilege of giving the annual Linder lecture on the same theme before the members of the Beatrix Potter Society.

The main collection of Beatrix's paintings of fungi is in the care of the Armitt Trust at Ambleside. Now for the first time modern technology has allowed the Armitt collection to be copied in colour so that prints can be studied closely in good light without risk of damage to the originals, and as a result Beatrix Potter's mycology can be studied in far greater depth. This new book will show that Findlay was right in his opinion that Beatrix Potter 'had the mind of a professional scientist and biologist – which is what she undoubtedly would have been had she lived in a later age – unless she had taken up archaeology!'

Such wealth of material becoming available calls for intensive, expert study over some time. This present contribution is therefore not an inclusive guide to the Armitt paintings, nor is it a field guide to fungi. It is a tribute to Beatrix Potter, mycologist, and Charles McIntosh, the Perthshire Naturalist who helped her.

55. *Coriolus versicolor*, Dunkeld, 1893. On the right Beatrix has painted a bracket turned over to show the under side.

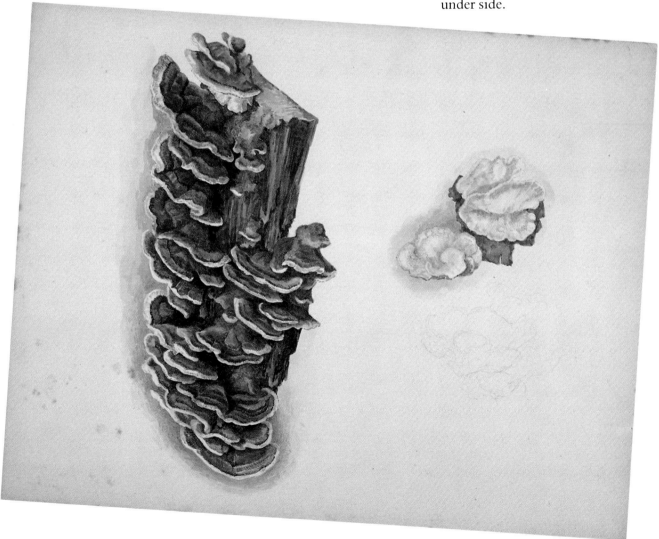

NAMING AND CLASSIFICATION OF FUNGI

Before discussing Beatrix Potter's mycology some explanation about the naming and classification of fungi is necessary, especially in view of modern developments. Fungus classification follows the binomial system introduced by the Swedish naturalist Linnaeus in the eighteenth century. Each fungus name is made up of two Latin (or occasionally Greek) words, the first indicating the genus or general group, the second a specific adjective. For example, Beatrix refers to the Velvet Shank by its Latin name *Agaricus velutipes*, where the first word gives the genus to which the fungus belongs and the second describes the particular species (*velutipes* meaning 'velvet foot').

In Beatrix's time a great many of the cap fungi with gills, 'mushrooms and toadstools', were all put together in the genus *Agaricus*. As knowledge of their structures and affinities increased, however, a number were transferred to new generic groups. Thus the two species mentioned in her first letter to Charles McIntosh, *Agaricus variabilis* and *Agaricus velutipes* (described on pages 67 and 68), are now called *Crepidotus variabilis* and *Flammulina velutipes*, the first new generic name from the Greek word for a slipper, *crepis*, and the other from the Latin, *flammula*, a flame. In both, the second part – the specific name – remains the same. In this book, if a fungus has a common, or English name, as with the Velvet Shank, it is used, but for the scientifically-minded

reader the Latin name as it appears in the Armitt Collection is also given, especially when we are sure, from her letters and her journal, that Beatrix herself used it. When a name has been replaced, the modern nomenclature, as accepted by the mycologists at the Royal Botanic Garden, Edinburgh, is added. Thus:

Velvet Shank (*Agaricus velutipes,* now *Flammulina velutipes*)

As Beatrix Potter refers in some detail to her study of fungi, the non-specialist reader may find useful the following simplified account of the structure and development of a toadstool.

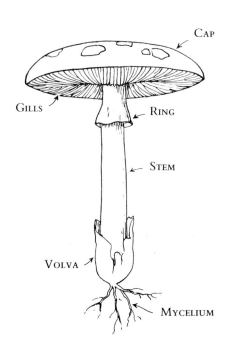

56. Structure of a toadstool

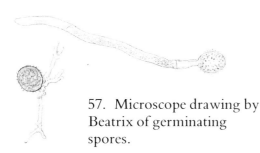

57. Microscope drawing by Beatrix of germinating spores.

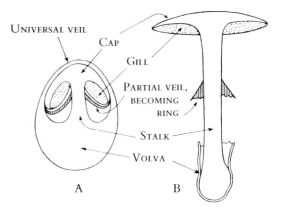

58. Development of a toadstool

Toadstools form many billions of spores which are to fungi what seeds are to green plants. Spores grow, or germinate, by pushing out a thin tube which soon becomes a long thread called a hypha (plural hyphae). The hyphae branch repeatedly to form a mass of fungal threads, a mycelium. This is what Beatrix called a 'mould'; it is the underground system from which the toadstool suddenly emerges, the mycelium having matted together in little knobs. The young toadstool may be protected by a cover called a veil. This breaks as the stem rises up and bits of it may stick to the outside of the 'umbrella' or cap. The white blobs on the Fly Agaric (*Amanita muscaria*) are the remains of this veil (see page 161).

In other toadstools only the young sporing parts are protected by a veil stretching from the stem to the edge of the cap. This is clearly shown in Beatrix's picture of Slippery Jack (see page 78). As the cap expands, the veil breaks up, exposing the spores, but it can still be seen as a ring on the stem. This also happens with commercial mushrooms. This second veil can be very thin and like a cobweb, when it is called a cortina, a curtain, as in *Cortinarius* (see page 85).

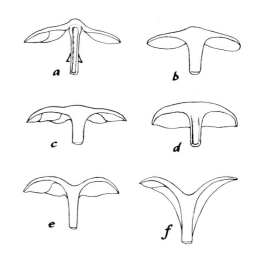

ATTACHMENT OF GILLS TO STEM
(A) FREE   (B) ADNEXED   (C) SINUATE
(D) ADNATE   (E) ADNATE WITH DECURRENT TOOTH
(F) DECURRENT

59. The attachment of gills to stem is an important feature in distinguishing different toadstools. In some the gills are clear of the stem, in others they run down it and others show all stages in between.

BEATRIX'S EARLY PAINTINGS OF FUNGI

The pictures on this page show some of the earliest of Beatrix Potter's paintings of fungi in the Armitt Collection. The Chanterelle (*Cantharellus cibarius*) was painted in September 1888 at Lingholm, in the Lake District. In December 1888 at the home of her grandfather Edmund Potter, Camfield Place in Hertfordshire, she painted the Wood Blewit (*Lepista nuda*) and the Russet Shank (*Collybia dryophila*). The Chanterelle picture has no background but for the others she wisely included the leafy substrate where they grew.

It was also in 1888 that Beatrix painted two fungus portraits which were to prove very important when in 1892 she met Charles McIntosh and compared notes with him. They were the Wood Hedgehog (*Hydnum repandum*) and the Common White Helvella (*Helvella crispa*). In her journal she describes the first 'with white spikes on the lower side' and the other 'like a spluttered candle'. The fact that she gives them no names either in Latin or English suggests that at this time she was not yet studying fungi seriously but was painting them mainly because of their beautiful colours and strange shapes. However, after her meeting with Charles McIntosh this would soon change.

60. Common White Helvella (*Helvella crispa*), the 'spluttered candle', Derwentwater, 1888.

60

61

62

62. Russet Shank (*Collybia dryophila*), Camfield Place, December 1888.

61. Wood Blewit (*Lepista nuda)*, Camfield Place, 1888.

63. Wood Hedgehog (*Hydnum repandum*), Lingholm, September 1888.

64. Chanterelle (*Cantharellus cibarius*), Lingholm, September 1888.

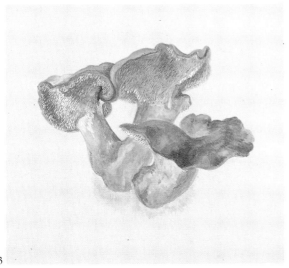

63

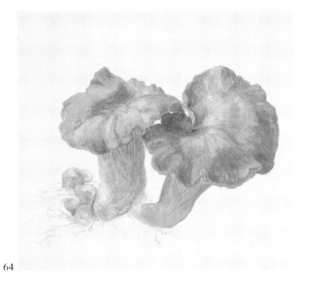

64

BEATRIX POTTER AND CHARLIE MCINTOSH

Charles McIntosh, known to his friends and to Beatrix throughout his life as Charlie, was a remarkable man. He was born in 1839 in a small country community in Scotland. His first job was in the local saw-mill in Inver but when an accident there resulted in the loss of the fingers of his left hand he became a postman, walking his beat of fifteen miles a day up and down the valley of the river Tay, one of the finest salmon rivers in Scotland.

Charlie had been interested in botany since his boyhood when his mother had given him the little book *Ferns and their Allies* by Dr Thomas Moore. His daily walks as a postman enabled him to pursue this study and he became extremely knowledgeable about all aspects of natural history. Ferns and mosses were his special subject. The first expert botanist he met was Dr F. Buchanan White, founder of the Perthshire Society for Natural Sciences, who persuaded Charlie to become an Associate Member. Charlie was too shy and not rich enough to attend the meetings in Perth or even the great Fungus Show in 1875 when the Cryptogamic Society of Scotland was set up. (Cryptogams include ferns, mosses, lichens and liverworts, as well as fungi.) However, at that Fungus Show some notable specimens were exhibited by 'C. McIntosh of Inver'. In 1877 a meeting of the Cryptogamic Society was held on Charlie's home ground, at Dunkeld, and this time he not only exhibited some splendid fungi and a collection of dried mosses, but also attended the meeting himself, met one of the foremost experts of the day, the Reverend John Stevenson of Glamis, and with his brother, entertained the company with their music on fiddle and cello.

The Potter family had been regularly travelling by train from London to spend the summer in Perthshire since Beatrix was a small girl and they first got to know Charlie as their postman. Beatrix wrote about him in her journal:

65. Charles McIntosh, the 'Perthshire Naturalist'.

65

It used to be an amusement to hop from puddle to puddle on the strides of Charlie's hob-nailed boots. I forget how many thousand miles he walked, some mathematical person reckoned it up. His successor has a tricycle, it will save his legs, but modern habits and machines are not calculated to bring out individuality or the study of Natural History. Country postmen, at all events in Scotland, are almost always men of intelligence with some special study. Probably the result of much solitary thinking and observation.

We have three letters from Rupert Potter to Charlie McIntosh. In 1887, Rupert wrote to him from 2 Bolton Gardens, Kensington, London, asking if he would like to have a copy of the newly-published two-volume book on fungi by the Reverend John Stevenson, *British Fungi (Hymenomycetes)*. Charlie obviously replied that he would accept this gift and the following two letters concern details of posting and delivery of that book and other volumes. They are written very formally in the third person:

> Mr Potter hopes the parcel will arrive in good condition. He is much pleased to learn that Mr McIntosh will value the Book as there is no one to whose knowledge in this region of learning Mr Potter could more suitably and pleasantly offer a book which unfortunately he himself does not understand.

The two volumes of Stevenson are still in the Museum and Art Gallery of Perth. They have the Potter family crest as a book-plate and are inscribed 'Charles McIntosh, Inver, Dunkeld, from Rupert Potter, London'. They have been much used and well annotated by Charlie.

The Potters spent the summer of 1892 at Birnam near Dunkeld in Perthshire and in Beatrix's journal entry of 29 October she relates how, just before the family returned to London, she managed to arrange a meeting

66. Beatrix Potter in her early twenties, photographed by her father.

with Charlie McIntosh to show him her fungus paintings.

> I have been trying all summer to speak with that learned but extremely shy man, it seemed stupid to take home the drawings without having shown them to him.
>
> Accordingly by appointment he came, with his soft hat, a walking stick, a little bundle, and very dirty boots, at five o'clock to the minute. He was quite painfully shy and uncouth at first, as though he was trying to swallow a muffin, and rolling his eyes about and mumbling.
>
> He was certainly pleased with my drawings and his judgement speaking to their accuracy in minute botanical points gave me infinitely more pleasure than that of critics who assume more, and know less than poor Charlie. He is a perfect dragon of erudition, and not gardener's Latin either.
>
> He had not been doing much amongst the moss lately he said modestly, he was 'studying slimes', fresh water algae. I asked him to sit down, his head being somewhere in the chandelier. I would not make fun of him for worlds, but he reminded me so much of a damaged lamp post. He warmed up to his favourite subject, his comments terse and to the point, and conscientiously accurate . . . When we discussed funguses he became quite excited and spoke with quite poetical feeling about their exquisite colours. He promised to send me some through the post, though I very much fear he will never have sufficient assurance to post them.

Charlie, however, did prove to have sufficient assurance and part of the ensuing correspondence between them still survives. It is these letters and the many paintings which she was making at the same time that give us a remarkable insight into Beatrix Potter's development as a natural historian.

Note

It appears that Beatrix often made two paintings of the
same subject and would send one to Charlie and keep the
second copy herself. The greater part of her own fungus
paintings are in the Armitt Collection, but those that she
gave to Charlie are now in the Perth Museum and Art
Gallery, and it is interesting to compare the very close
similarity of the same picture in the Armitt and Perth
versions. The fungi she mentions showing to Charlie at
their meeting in 1892, the Wood Hedgehog and the
Common White Helvella, appear together on one sheet
in the Perth collection and it seems likely that she gave
this actual sheet to Charlie on that occasion. The separate
versions now in the Armitt Collection were kept as her
own record. The originals of the Dunkeld Letters from
Rupert and Beatrix Potter were bequeathed by Miss
MacIntosh to the National Library of Scotland, Edinburgh.

67. The sheet showing the
Wood Hedgehog (above)
and the Common White
Helvella (below), dated
1888, which is now in the
collection of the Perth
Museum and Art Gallery.

67

THE DUNKELD LETTERS

The earliest letter we have from Beatrix to Charlie is dated 10 December 1892 and, like her father, she writes in a very formal style.[1]

> Dec. 10th 92
> 2 Bolton Gardens
> S.W.

Miss Potter has sent off the drawings by parcel post and hopes Mr McIntosh will think them sufficiently accurate to be worth his acceptance.

The last plants were particularly beautiful, Agaricus variabilis is almost like a pansy and A. velutipes also very handsome. A curious thing has happened to the piece of broom on which the latter was growing. It was put away in a tin canister and forgotten, and now another species of fungus has sprung up. It is a pale straw colour, grown entirely in the dark and there are nearly 100 'fingers', the longest measure 1¼ inch. Miss Potter wonders whether it grows out of doors at this season or whether it is brought out by the heat of the room? It was about this size when first observed but being moved into hot cupboard near the kitchen chimney, it puffed out in a very odd shape. The last shoots that have grown are the same size all the way up. Miss Potter supposes the plants are over for this season, judging by the weather reported in the Perthshire paper, but when Mr McIntosh can get any more she will be glad to draw them. It is a real pleasure to copy them, they are such lovely colours. The moss is more trouble on account of being magnified, and

---

[1] The transcripts of these letters reproduce Beatrix and Charlie's own spelling and punctuation. For consistency, therefore, Latin names are not printed in italic within the letters; italic type is used only where Beatrix or Charlie underlined a word for emphasis.

Miss Potter thinks she will keep any drawings of moss, to add to her set. She has drawn most of the fungi *twice*. It might be well to mark the rarest plant in each parcel (or that could not be replaced) so that it might be painted first. Stereum purpureum went mouldy during fogs. Agaricus fragrans is curiously strong and *pleasant*. Miss Potter trust Mr McIntosh will never send a horrid plant like a white stick with a loose cap, which smells exactly like a dead sheep! She went to look at a fine specimen but could not find courage to draw it.

Beatrix's use of the Latin names here suggests that Charlie was supplying them along with the specimens.

Beatrix mentions in this letter that she is drawing mosses 'magnified'. Both she and Charlie had microscopes. We know from her drawing of the wing

The comment on the first *Agaricus* (now *Crepidotus* species) being like a pansy is very apt as the gills face upward rather than being concealed under the cap. More mundane mycologists thought these faces looked like slippers (*crepidotus* = slipper).

This painting of *Crepidotus mollis* was made by Beatrix in 1895.

68

69

70

The second fungus mentioned is the Velvet Shank (*Agaricus velutipes*, now *Flammulina velutipes*). The picture above (69), dated November 1892, shows the Velvet Shank in full growth. The fungus appears best in winter (see the drawings by Sophia Armitt made in December, page 33) so would be very easy for Charlie to send by post to London. It apparently arrived in good condition. It has been all too common in Britain in recent years as it grows on elms killed by Dutch elm disease.

The mysterious 'other species of fungus' in the canister was only the Velvet Shank growing in the dark! Beatrix made a little drawing of it in colour on the sheet above (70), matching the sketch in her letter to Charlie. The other two drawings on the sheet show the 'handsome' *Crepidotus* above, and *Plicaturiopsis crispa* below.

canister & forgotten, and now another ab
species of fungus has sprung up - but
It is a pale straw colour, grown one
entirely in the dark, and there are or
nearly 100 'fingers',
the longest measure
1¼ inch - Miss Potter
wonders whether it
grows out of doors at
this season or whether it is brou
out by the heat of the room?

scales of a butterfly (see page 145) that in 1887 she had one with magnification about 200 times. By 1896 she also had a lens giving higher magnification, about 600 times (⅙th objective). In her journal for 1896 she tells how this precious lens fell among the cinders and was scratched. But on a visit to Becks (good microscope makers) she 'got a splendid ⅛th lens'. This would magnify slightly more than the old lens. We can calculate that generally the 'high power' of Beatrix's drawings may be taken as about ×600. Some of her drawings have a scale added or '×600' written beside the picture. Her 'low power' would be about ×200 and she probably had a very good hand-lens which, coupled with her excellent eyesight for close-up work, gave her a magnification of ×20.

Charlie had to 'save up' for his microscope; it was made by Hartnach and cost him £7. He had a scale in the eyepiece so he could measure spores easily and accurately. He bought it in 1887 and his brother James said, 'After that the microscope was always on the table and he was never done working with it.' James took the photograph of Charlie with his microscope on page 62. Beatrix had hers in Birnam in 1892 when they met, so doubtless this would have been another topic for discussion between them.

71

Quite recently another sheet of Beatrix's fungus drawings has come to light in a London private collection which is also connected with her early collaboration with Charlie. The sheet (72) shows two little fragile toadstools and has the date 'Dunkeld 92', the word 'parcel' and the name *Stereum purpureum* in faint pencil. It is therefore extremely likely that these specimens were sent from Dunkeld by Charlie in the very first parcel already discussed even though they are not mentioned in Beatrix's letter of 10 December.

Beatrix tried to name them using her 'Stevenson' and wrote the names in ink. The larger group at the bottom of the sheet she thought was *Agaricus (Galera) hypnorum*, a fungus which grows among the moss *Hypnum*. Expert opinion, however, is that it is too robust and the stems too thick to be what is now called *Galerina hypnorum*; the olivaceous tints and the way the gills are attached would suggest the equally common *Galerina mniophila*, whose specific name again comes from the name of a moss, *Mnium*.

The other little toadstool Beatrix labelled *Agaricus (Omphalia) campanella* but the fungus depicted is too pale for that species. It is probably a member of the group of Omphalia-like Mycenas, although the clustered arrangement of the stems in the fungus shown is rather unusual in this group. In 1893, at Eastwood, Dunkeld, Beatrix did paint an *Omphalina, Omphalina pseudoandrosacea* (see page 116). This is a particularly interesting species as we now know that it forms a lichen, a point which is discussed later.

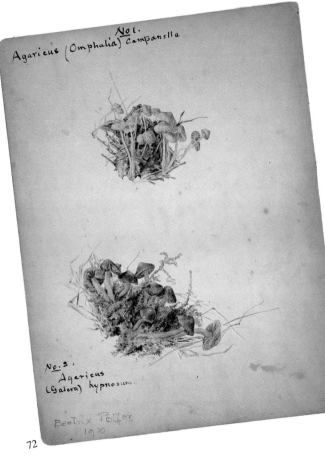

72

The 'horrid plant like a white stick with a loose cap which smells exactly like a dead sheep' is undoubtedly the Stinkhorn (*Phallus impudicus*); judging by the evidence available to us Beatrix never did 'find courage to draw it'.

The first part of the next letter, probably written in autumn 1893, is missing.

2 Bolton Gardens
S.W.

and ask if he would tell me, or you, the name of a book that would contain the other funguses, puff-balls, Helvella, etc. If there is one on the same plan as Dr Stevenson's I would prefer it. I have been looking carefully through part of the drawings at the museum. There are a number of portfolios with drawings and printed plates which one may see at any time, but no one to give any information apparently. They have about 30 per cent of the funguses, rather more of the smaller divisions. There are the originals of the illustrations in Dr S's [Stevenson's] book, by Mr Worthington Smith. The drawing of Strobilomyces is dated Ludlow 1868. I did not hear whether it came up again. They are extremely anxious to have a specimen to put in methylated spirit. If Mr McIntosh finds it again he had better present it; it is a great curiosity, but they take no interest whatever in funguses at large.

All the plants we were doubtful about are marked ? especially between B[*oletus*] chrysenteron and subtomentosus, B. scaber and versipellis; and varieties of luridus. B. cyanescens (mine) is like their B. pachypus, but I think there must be some confusion, as pachypus does not turn dark blue. Hygrophorus coccineus and puniceus also?? They seem to vary much in colour but it depends on the white foot of the stem. I have not looked at the cortinariuses yet. I think I will ask at Kew Gardens some day, whether there is anyone there who knows more about the names.

The museum Beatrix had been visiting was London's Natural History Museum which, in 1893, was still only a department of the British Museum in Bloomsbury. This

73. Old Man of the Woods
(*Strobilomyces floccopus*),
drawn *in situ* at Eastwood,
Dunkeld, 3 September 1893.

73

was a stormy period in its development *vis-à-vis* its parent body in Bloomsbury and also because it had recently been suggested that the Natural History Museum's botanical collections should be transferred to the Royal Botanic Gardens at Kew. Natural history without botany is a curious idea! This was also the time when living plant specimens were not welcome, either at the Natural History Museum or at Kew. At the former the procedure was to put fungi in spirit, in pickle, while Kew preferred material that had been dried and pressed and could then be matched with herbarium specimens. As we have seen (page 36), Sophia Armitt submitted herbarium specimens to Kew, although even she got little satisfaction.

Strobilomyces strobilaceus (now *Strobilomyces floccopus*) has a common name although it is a very rare fungus in Scotland. It is the 'Old Man of the Woods'. Its Latin name comes from its similarity to a Scots pine cone (*strobilus* = pine cone). This fungus was found in the grounds of Eastwood House, Dunkeld, by Beatrix while she was staying there in the summer of 1893. On 3 September she made three paintings of it, two of which are now in the Armitt Collection and one in Perth Museum. We have written evidence that Charlie sent a specimen of the fungus to the Reverend John Stevenson at Glamis for verification and he replied that it had only been found once before in Scotland in 1889, near Crieff, Perthshire. It appears, however, that Beatrix already knew the identity of this rare fungus that even Charlie had not previously seen. Recently Mrs Joan Duke, of Troutbeck, Ambleside, found a strange painting of a fungus by Beatrix which was identified on the back as *Strobilomyces strobilaceus* from Crieff and dated 1889. The Cryptogamic Society of Scotland held a meeting in Crieff that year. Beatrix was certainly not there but one of the party, a Drummond Hay, was then living in Dunkeld. Did he bring the fungus to Beatrix to paint? At any rate, the painting now in the Museum and Art Gallery of Perth, courtesy of Mrs Duke, is a portrait of the first specimen found in Scotland. The paintings Beatrix made at Eastwood in 1893 of fresh material are far better.

The final paragraph shows that she already knew her fungi better than the professionals at the Natural History Museum. A year had passed since her meeting with Charlie and she had reached a stage when she could discuss the precise points which distinguished one fungus from another, and was quite ready to take on the museum experts concerning the identification of *Boletus* and *Hygrophorus* species.

74. *Boletus chrysenteron* is correctly named. Its common name is the Red-cracked Bolete. It was painted at Holehird, Windermere, in August 1895.   74

75. *Boletus subtomentosus* has now been renamed by Dr Watling of the Royal Botanic Garden, Edinburgh, as a new species, *Boletus porosporus*. This painting was dated by Beatrix September 9, 1893, at Eastwood.   75

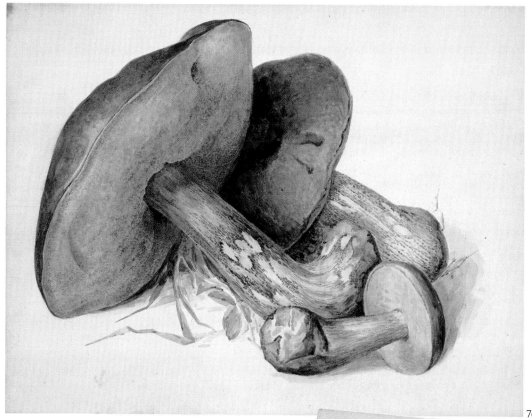

76

76. *Boletus scaber* has been put into a new genus *Leccinum*, so the modern Latin name for this fungus is *Leccinum scabrum*. It retains its common name in English, Brown Birch Bolete, being found with birch trees. This painting was made at Dunkeld in August 1983.

Boletus versipellis, the Orange Birch Bolete, similarly now becomes *Leccinum versipelle*. An important distinguishing feature of some boletes is their change of colour when broken or bruised. This is clearly shown in the painting of *versipelle* (77). The specific name means changing skin, the cap changing from light to dark orange while the flesh and stem can even change to blue when cut, as in this picture.

77

78

79

78. The painting made at Eastwood in 1893 was wrongly identified as *Boletus cyanescens*; it is in fact *Boletus badius*, the Bay Bolete, named for its bay colour. 79 was identified in the Armitt Collection as *Boletus luridus*, but it is *Boletus erythropus*, the Red Leg. It was collected at Lennel, Coldstream, in 1894.

80. *Boletus pachypus* has now changed its name to *Boletus calopus* (from 'stout foot' to 'beautiful'). Beatrix painted this picture at Eastwood in September 1893. As she said, it does not 'turn dark blue'. The specimens at the museum being in pickle, the colours would be obscured.

80

81

82

Beatrix was also right with her point about the difference between the two 'Wax Caps', now called *Hygrocybe coccinea* and *Hygrocybe punicea*. *Coccinea* is the Scarlet Wax Cap and *punicea* the Crimson or Blood-red Wax Cap, difficult colours to differentiate. In the painting she made in October 1894 at Coldstream (81) she shows the distinctive white base of the stem of *puniceus* as mentioned in this letter. *Hygrocybe coccinea* (82), from Lingholm, was painted in October 1897.

83. The Cep (*Boletus edulis*) from Blelham Tarn, August 1895.

MORE MYCOLOGY

The concept of 'families' in fungi, as in flowering plants, is a recent development in mycology. The two families discussed in the above letter, *Boletaceae* and *Hygrophoraceae* or boletes and waxy ones, were of great interest to both Beatrix and Charlie.

THE BOLETES

The boletes have their spores in tiny tubes, not on gills like mushrooms, so they have a spongy mass of pores under the cap. The best known of this group is the Penny Bun or Cep (*Boletus edulis*), used in commercial 'mushroom' soup.

Boletus has now been sub-divided into several genera of which one, *Leccinum*, has already been mentioned. One of its distinguishing features, visible even to the naked eye, is its stem with distinct black or dark brown scales as shown in Beatrix's painting of the Orange Birch Bolete. In *Boletus* the stem has a network or pattern of faint lines as in Beatrix's portrait of the Bay Bolete (see page 75).

In both *Boletus* and *Leccinum* the cap can be viscid, sticky, but not glutinous. The really glutinous ones are now called *Suillus* (*suillus* = pig), and at the Loch of the Lowes, Dunkeld, Beatrix painted one of the best known, Slippery Jack, *Suillus luteus* (*luteus* = yellow).

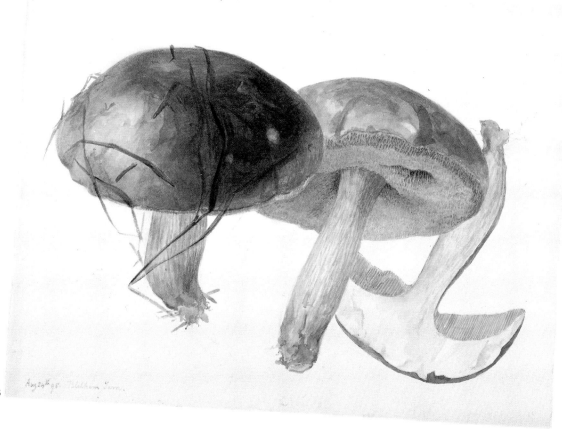

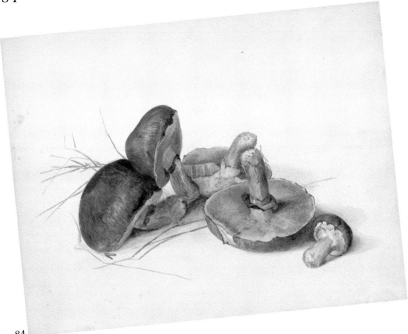

84. Slippery Jack (*Suillus luteus*) from Loch of the Lowes, Dunkeld, September 1893.

84

Long after Beatrix had lost touch with Charlie she put 'Boletus' into her unpublished sequel to *The Fairy Caravan*. The character Tuppenny noted one 'sitting out in the sun, drying its sticky cap' which is just what a member of the new genus *Suillus* would do.

These differential characteristics may seem rather vague but mycologists of today also use microscopic and chemical features to identify fungi by methods which were not available a hundred years ago. The Old Man of the Woods is in the same fungus family as the boletes. But although there are many different species in *Suillus, Boletus* and *Leccinum*, there is only the one in Europe in the genus *Strobilomyces*.

Dr Roy Watling of the Royal Botanic Garden, Edinburgh, who has made a special study of the boletes, has been able to rename several of the Armitt paintings.

THE WAXY ONES

In Beatrix's time these were all included in *Hygrophorus*, the water bearers. Now those with waxy gills are called *Hygrocybe*, literally, 'wax head', while those waxy all over remain in *Hygrophorus*. The Parrot Toadstool, *Hygrocybe psittacina* was painted several times by Beatrix (see page 175). The portrait below (85) of *Hygrocybe citrinovirens* was painted at Lingholm, Keswick, in 1898.

85

Whereas *Hygrocybe* prefers grassy places, *Hygrophorus* is found in woodland sites. One of them, *Hygrophorus pustulatus*, was of special interest to Charlie. He found it in a plantation of spruce at Dunkeld and in 1909 was credited with being the first person to record it in Britain. But Beatrix had also painted a Waxy One in 1893 or 1894 which she thought was the species *fusco-albus* (below). The experts' opinion is that it is indeed *Hygrophorus pustulatus*. So the credit for the first recording of this rare northern fungus should, after all, go to Beatrix!

86.   *Hygrophorus pustulatus* from Hatchednize Wood, October 1894.

87.   *Hygrocybe laeta* in grass, Holehird and Langdale, September 1895.

WINTER 1893/1894 – COLLABORATION

The next letter from Beatrix to Charlie is dated 19 November with no year. It was probably written from London in November 1893 and her reference to being at Torquay 'last year' should be read as 'last spring'. The Potters had once again spent the summer in Perthshire, staying this time at Eastwood, Dunkeld. We know very little about this holiday for although Beatrix describes the 1892 visit in great detail in her journal, there is, mysteriously, a complete blank in the journal for the holiday at Eastwood in 1893. It is very likely, however, that the meeting between Beatrix and Charlie in 1892 was followed by more active cooperation on mycology in

88

88. This picture was painted at Eastwood on 25 September 1893. The three upright fungi are Butter Cap or Greasy Tough Shank (*Collybia butyracea*) and the one lying down is *Collybia* species.

89. The painting below of an unidentified species (left) and *Amanita citrina* (right) is dated Eastwood, 15 August 1893. The original has faded badly.

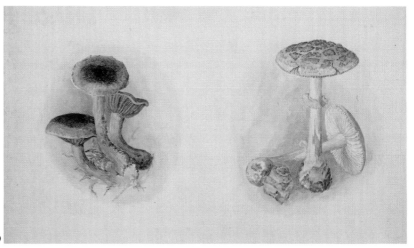

89

1893. Many of Charlie's favourite places for finding interesting species are recorded on Beatrix's drawings from this period. One was the sawmill at Inver, the village where Charlie lived. Another was the deserted village, Tomgarrow, on the moor in Strathbraan. But whether Beatrix did her fungus-hunting alone or not her technique for painting was already showing the results of her collaboration with Charlie.

> I have not had A [*garicus*] mitis before, you sent Panus stipticus once. Most of the cortinarius was unbroken and has kept well. The only unfortunate parcel has been the fungus 'A' which was in small chips, which I regretted as it must have been a pretty group, to judge by the stalks.
>
> I think I have made rather a successful drawing of Cantharellus umbonatus, I shall be more careful now that I have the book.
>
> I wish I had had the book sooner, for most of my drawings might have been made more accurate, without extra trouble, if I had understood anything about the distinctions. Dr Stevenson's book is rather stiff reading, but I understand it sufficiently to find it extremely interesting. I don't know if I shall ever get the classification into my head but I hope to master the glossary before next season. I have found this handbook of some assistance, but I have not seen the models yet, as I have had a cold. There are several things which puzzle me completely, but I will study a bit longer before troubling you with any questions. There is one thing to be said for my drawings, they can easily be washed out and corrected being in watercolour; the gills are the weak point.
>
> I think I found some of 'Myxomycetes' (p. 80) at Torquay on a paling last year, like large white slugs, but no skin and disagreeable to touch. I think I had better keep to the Hymenomycetes at present; there are quite enough of them.

It is not clear which book Beatrix is referring to at the beginning of the third paragraph, but the 'handbook' she mentions later was the guide to models of fungi made by a mycologist called Sowerby to show the public which fungi could be safely eaten and which were poisonous. After his death in 1844 the models were donated to the Natural History Museum. Beatrix would certainly recognise the outline drawings in the guide as they were the work of Worthington G. Smith, a good mycologist as well as a commercial artist, who also illustrated Dr Stevenson's *British Fungi (Hymenomycetes)*. The category Hymenomycetes used by Dr Stevenson includes most of the larger mushrooms and toadstools.

The slime moulds, the Myxomycetes, turn up again in the sequel to *The Fairy Caravan*: 'I know Mixomycetes [*sic*] walks about; I have seen him go from one end of a log to another', which is just what slime moulds can do.

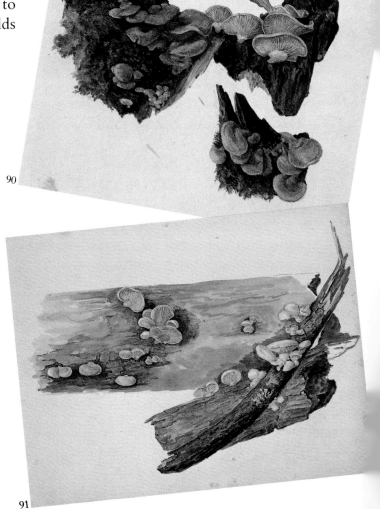

90

The two species *mitis* and *stipticus* are now in the genus *Panellus*. Both are found in winter, so it would be easy for Charlie to get material to send to London. *Mitis* indicates it is mild to taste whereas *stipticus* is styptic or astringent. We have a drawing (90) Beatrix made of *stipticus* when she was first sent this fungus from Dunkeld in November 1892. The picture of *mitis* (91) is dated December 1894, also from Dunkeld. The portraits of these fungi are remarkably good considering they were posted to Beatrix. It is important to bear this in mind when comparing one portrait with another.

91

92. *Cantharellus umbonatus* (now *Cantharellula umbonata*), the little Chanterelle with a knob on top she definitely painted very successfully. The version of this portrait in the Perth Museum is undoubtedly that referred to in this letter and was dated by Beatrix herself 19 November 1893.

92

We have now no means of knowing how many letters Charlie may have written but only two survive. This first one is dated 10 January 1894, from Inver, Dunkeld. It was found at the Armitt Trust in a copy of Coates' biography of Charlie, *A Perthshire Naturalist*. His style of address is very formal. (Beatrix had by now stopped calling him 'Mr McIntosh' in her letters but subsequently never managed to address him at all!)

> Miss Potter
> Madam
> I received the fungus sent. I could not get the spores, and although it cannot be said to be white, yet I think it must be Merulius corium. I've seen it in this district but without the hymenium [the spore-bearing part] so I'm glad to get a fertile plant. I also got a British Museum Guide to the funguses, which you kindly sent. It is very good. I am sorry there

was so little to send you since you left. A good many funguses appeared but from one cause or another an entire specimen was not to be got. Since you have begun to study the physiology of the funguses you seem to see your drawings of them as defective in regard to the gills, but you can make them more perfect as botanical drawings by making separate sketches of sections showing the attachment of the gills, the stem, if it be hollow or otherwise, or any other details that would show the characteristics of the plant more distinctly.

Yours when sent
Charles Macintosh

Charlie's writing is not easy to read but this seems to be his greeting. His form of signature also varies. The second letter we have from him is signed Charles 'McIntosh'.

The British Museum Guide which Beatrix 'kindly sent' would be the guide to the Sowerby models which Beatrix mentions in her previous letter.

It is, however, the last part of the letter that is so important. Beatrix had written of her own work, 'The gills are the weak point.' Now she was given the directive she needed and the subsequent paintings show how well she followed it. Modern mycologists still need these points – the attachment of the gills to the stem and the appearance of the stem cut down from the cap – to identify fungi. Reproduction of the colours was no problem for her and the inclusion of these details in her drawings enables the portraits to be identified today.

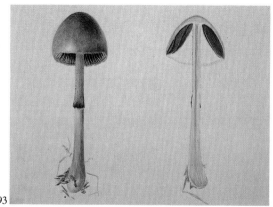

93. Beatrix found the Dung Mottle Gill (*Panaeolus semiovatus*) at Smailholm Tower near Lennel and painted it with the long section showing the stem and gills on 25 September 1894. The black ring on the stem is all that remains of the veil that protected the spores.

93

THE LENNEL HOLIDAY 1894

The next letter is undated but, from the context, it was
very probably sent while Beatrix was on holiday in 1894.
That year, although the Potters again went to Scotland,
they did not stay in Perthshire but in the Scottish Border
country at Lennel near Coldstream. During this visit
Beatrix found and painted many interesting fungi, and
makes frequent references to
fungus-hunting in her journal.

> Sunday, September 30th – Was overtaken with
> funguses, especially Hygrophorus. Found a lovely
> pink one. They begin to come in
> crowds, exasperating to leave.

94. Thanks to this painting of the
'lovely pink one' we can confirm that
she found the rare waxy Pink Meadow
Cap (*Hygrophorus calyptraeformis*), named
for its hood-like head (*calyptra* = hood
or cap).

94

> Monday, October 1st – These woods about here are
> a sort where one can get lost directly, black firs, and
> going in I found heather, bracken, and a large
> broken log. There was a great growth of crisp
> yellow Peziza in the moss, and a troop of gigantic
> Cortinarius. I brought away the largest, eight inches
> across and weighing just under a pound.

The name *Cortinarius* comes from the
'cortina' or little veil which in young
specimens stretch from the cap to the
stem, concealing the gills (see page 59).
Sometimes these are called the Curtain
fungi from this veil. In the painting of
Cortinarius species (95), made at Lennel
in October 1894, the cortina can be most
clearly seen on the little fungus at the
bottom.

95

Saturday, August 18th – Went again to the wood near Hatchednize suspecting funguses from the climate, and was rewarded, what should be an ideal heavenly dream of the toadstool eaters . . . The fungus starred the ground apparently in thousands, a dozen sorts in sight at once, and such specimens,

Her painting of this Spike Cap (*Gomphidius glutinosus*), from Hatchednize Wood, 18 and 19 August 1894, includes young as well as mature fructifications. The long section of the stem and the veil are drawn on a separate sheet – so as not to upset the symmetry of the group?

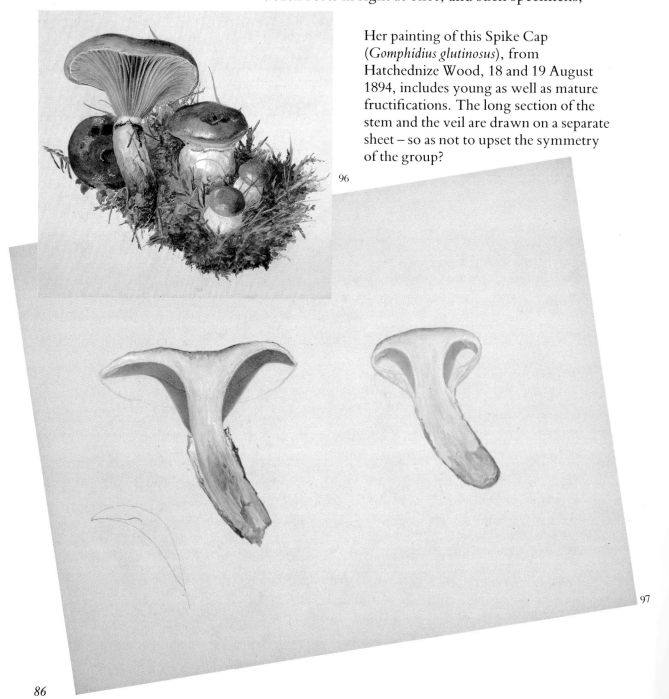

96

97

which I have noted before in this neighbourhood. I found upwards of twenty sorts in a few minutes, Cortinarius and the handsome Lactarius deliciosus being conspicuous, and joy of joys, the spiky Gomphidius glutinosus, a round, slimy purple head among the moss, which I took up carefully with my old cheese-knife, and turning over saw the slimy veil. There is extreme complacency in finding a totally new species for the first time.

Beatrix was obviously corresponding with Charlie during this holiday. An entry in the journal on 5 October reads: 'Had rather interesting communication from C.M., anent [about] Hygrophoruses.' The existing letter from her to him is as follows:

I am sorry that A[*garicus*] spadiceus [now *Psathyrella spadicea*] turned out to be common but it is very handsome in any case. I suppose A. paedidus would be about as good as A. decastes. If Dr Stevenson were not infallible one would say it was more like the description of *decastes*. I have made some very bad guesses but had chosen the right names for the Hygrophorus, except *nitratus* which I thought was *unguinosus* because it never seems to have any 'strong nitrous smell', but if it is really nitratus I think I may have found the larger form as well, much thicker with broad crumpled gills. Both came up sparingly and I stupidly missed getting a drawing. There has been a good deal of Helvella single plants and two half rings at the edge of a pasture, most curious looking. A [*garicus*] personatus appeared whiter than ever, and also the ordinary colour growing near it. The large cortinarius has not come up again properly. I got very large ones nearly rotten in Birgham Wood, the largest 8 inches across, weighing over 15 oz, think the same fungus. I had some better specimens of H[*ygrophorus*] puniceus but all rather dry. It must be splendid in wet weather. They were solitary in coarse grass with rushes.

98

In Dr Stevenson's book there is only one British record of what he called 'decastes', in Wales, so if he had accepted Beatrix's specimen as *decastes* this would have been the first record of it in Scotland; hence the slight sense of disappointment when she asks if '*paedidus* would be about as good as *decastes*'. However, Dr Stevenson's infallibility may be more open to question than Beatrix thought.

Decastes and *paedidus* are now classified in different genera, *decastes* becoming *Lyophyllum*: some experts altogether dismiss *paedidus* as a distinct species. There is, however, one point on which the authorities all agree – *Lyophyllum decastes* is very variable. The painting above is now identified as *Lyophyllum decastes*. There is a very similar one in Perth dated 29 September 1894, so it may have been sent to Charlie from Lennel at about this time. Perhaps Dr Stevenson should have accepted Beatrix and Charlie's 'decastes' identification after all!

99

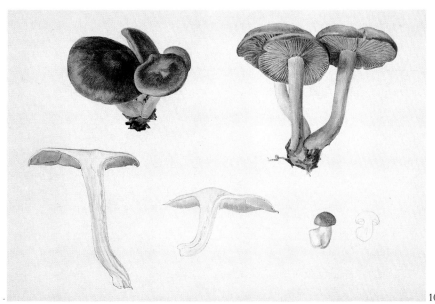

100

100. This painting, dated September 1894, is now identified as a species of *Lyophyllum*.

We may imagine that in Dunkeld in 1893 Beatrix and Charlie would discuss how to identify different fungi. Beatrix's comment about this one not having a 'strong nitrous smell' is significant, as smell can be a distinctive feature. Had she ventured to taste it she might have remarked on the absence of the repulsive, soapy taste typical of *nitratus*. This portrait (101) of the true *nitratus* (now *Hygrocybe nitrata*) was painted in November 1896.

101

102. *Agaricus personatus* is the Common Blewit or Blue Stalk, now *Lepista saeva*, an excellent mushroom for eating. Blewit is the old English name for blue one. Beatrix found this lighter coloured specimen in Lennel in September 1894, although the 'ordinary colour' she mentions in her letter is blue. One of her first paintings of fungi, made in 1888, was of the Wood Blewit, *Lepista nuda* (see page 61).

102

CHARLIE'S SECOND LETTER

The story of the survival of the next letter is extraordinary. It was found in a copy of Ramsay's *Physical Geography of Great Britain* which had belonged to Beatrix. She had bought the book and written her name in it with the date 'July 1894'. There is little doubt that she had it with her later that year in the Scottish Border country at Lennel, since her journal for that holiday is full of geological observations. In 1946 a Mr Nixon from Torquay in Devon, on holiday in the Lake District, bought the book in a secondhand bookshop in Ambleside, took it back to Torquay and donated it, as a useful reference book on geology, to the extensive library of the Torquay Natural History Society. In 1984, during a reorganisation of the library, it was noticed for the first time that the book had belonged to Beatrix Potter. It was referred to Mr John Clegg, former Curator of the Museum at Torquay, a fine naturalist and expert on Beatrix Potter. He found, tucked into the book, this letter from Charles McIntosh and several photographs of the Potters, including one of Beatrix sitting outside Kent's Cavern in Torquay where the family had their spring holiday in 1893. The book and its contents were placed in the care of the Armitt Trust; the photograph was returned to the Torquay Natural History Society library.

The letter is undated but it seems likely it was written in the autumn of 1894 about specimens Beatrix had sent from Lennel.

Inver
Dunkeld

Miss Potter
Madam
The large fungus sent in the hamper is a Cortinarius belonging to the Phlegmacium tribe, and the Cliduchii division, and but for its stem which is not cylindrical and has got tawny I would take it to be

C. turmalis, but am not at all sure of it. If any of the three first Cliduchii it is a good find.

If you could get it in the young stage before the gills had changed colour, and the stem and Cortina had been dusted with the spores, you would be able to name it. The only other like it is C. multiformis.

The scaly Agaricus growing on Ash is A. squarrosus. The var. vahlii of Agaricus aureus is appearing where I found it before. I hope to get a good plant of it soon.

Yours when sent
C. McIntosh

Phlegmacium is now the name of a sub-genus within *Cortinarius* whose species are notoriously difficult to distinguish from one another. Beatrix's painting of a *Cortinarius* from Lennel is shown on page 85. Perhaps this is the specimen she sent to Charlie.

The fungus Charlie called 'var. *vahlii* of *Agaricus aureus*' (now *Phaeolepiota aurea*, the 'golden one'), was special to him. In 1875, when the Cryptogamic Society of Scotland was founded in Perth, a fungus show was held attended by many eminent mycologists. One was the Rev. M. J. Berkeley, considered the 'father' of British mycology. He was very impressed by the splendid specimen of *Agaricus aureus* exhibited by Charlie and asked whether he might have another sent to his home in England. In Dr Stevenson's working copy of his own book *British Fungi* there is a holograph note, '1875, Inver Dunkeld'. It is a rare fungus.

103. Beatrix made a painting of the 'golden one', dated Inver, July 1896. It is assessed by modern experts as a poor specimen.

103

1895 – LONDON AND THE LAKES

This letter was probably written from London in the winter of 1895, judging from the reference to the 'Lennel' fungus.

I copied these outlines of A. cortinarius turmalis from Mr Worthington Smith's, at the Natural History Museum; I don't think it is very like either your plant or mine, more like the very slimy yellow one which I did not send, which came up, from the first, with a longer stem. Your specimen from Murthly was very curious with the solid white stem; I hope you will find it again next season. I don't think it was the same as the Lennel one, the silky fibre was different on the top and the white trama.

There are about 40 large sheets of drawings, life size, framed, by Mr W. Smith, including the illustrations in Dr Stevenson's book, to the end of the Agarics only. The outlines are beautifully drawn, but they don't show the texture and they are very coarsely coloured. There is no drawing of A. terreus. I thought my old drawing (but I am not at all sure about it) was the same as a fungus which was very common in beech woods at Coldstream, which I supposed was A. terreus, but I think there was more than one sort. It was sometimes quite matted on the top and the gills varied; there must be several very similar to each other, but I never saw one with a yellow tinge like A. portenosus [*portentosus*]. It was commonly rather dry, inclined to split, growing rather flat, in clumps. I don't know if there is anyone at the museum to explain about funguses, but I think they have a very poor collection, about 3 dozen British and foreign in bottles or dried. Sowerby's clay models are merely curiositie

I see some funguses which may possibly be A. pleurotus ulmarius but not much chance of getting at them, unless they fall down when rotten.

A. longicaudus is very like A. spadaceus [*spadiceus*] but has a slight bulb. A. imbricatus and A. vaccinus look like yours. A. aureus, similar, but a single plant of enormous size.

Before commenting on the fungi mentioned in this letter it is worthwhile considering Beatrix's assessment of the illustrations of fungi in the Natural History Museum. Worthington G. Smith has already been mentioned (see page 82) as a notable mycologist and the commercial artist who illustrated both the guide to Sowerby's fungus models (dismissed here by Beatrix as 'merely curiosities') and Dr Stevenson's book *British Fungi*. His 'beautifully drawn' pictures are reproduced in black and white in Dr Stevenson's book but Beatrix's comment on the colour of the originals, 'very coarsely coloured', is significant when one realises how splendidly she was drawing *and* painting the fungi at this time.

104

104. 'My old drawing' could well be the one she made at Dunkeld, on 13 September 1893. Expert opinion is that this is not a portrait of *Tricholoma terreum* but *Tricholoma sciodes*.

The 'slimy yellow' *Cortinarius* mentioned could be related to the one shown on page 85 painted at Lennel in October 1894. The painting right (105), dated Dunkeld, November 1893, is probably *Cortinarius cinnamomeobadius*. Note the righthand stem cut down and showing the attachment of gills to stem. The species of *Cortinarius* are notoriously difficult to differentiate as Charlie indicated in his letter of autumn 1894.

105

106. Beatrix painted *Agaricus portentosus* (now *Tricholoma portentosum*, a 'monstrous one') on 16 October 1894. Here the details of the cap are included but in pencil alongside two fructifications in full colour.

106

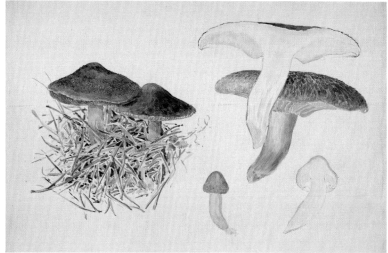

107

The sketch below (108) is captioned by Beatrix herself *imbricatus* and dated 26 September 1894. The cap has the appearance of tiles on a roof, hence 'imbricate'. This fungus is now in the genus *Tricholoma* which takes its name from the hairs or filaments (Greek *thrix* = hair, *loma* = fringe) on the margin of the cap. These are just visible in the painting. The detailed painting (107) was made at a later date in 1901 at Lingholm.

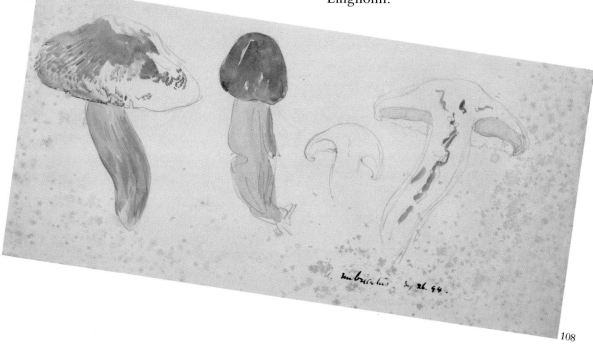

108

The 'long-tailed one', *longicaudus*, is now in the genus *Hebeloma*, the fringe-like veil only being present in certain young fructifications (*hebe* = youth). It has a slight bulb at the base of the stem as shown in Beatrix's sketch in her letter. The stem is so long she drew it in two parts!

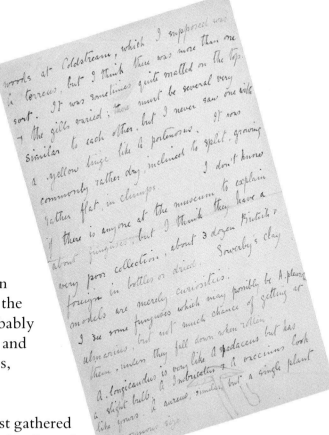

109

In 1895 the Potters spent the summer not in Scotland but in Holehird, Windermere, in the Lake District. This scrap of paper was probably sent to Charlie in the course of the holiday and accompanied fungus specimens or, perhaps, Beatrix's latest batch of paintings.

Is not this Boletus Granulatus? When first gathered the young plants were very slimy and had yellowish milky drops on the pores and stem. It was in a thin wood, scotch fir and larch, also poor specimens of B. laricinus and Gomphidius glutinosus and G. viscidus.
   Gracilis? It is different to the large ones at Coldstream.

As already noted, the boletes especially interested Beatrix. There are no fewer than twenty-eight paintings of them in the Armitt Collection. One of them (110) is a fine representation of the species *granulatus*, now *Suillus granulatus*, painted at Holehird on 2 August 1895. Her remark in the letter about it being found in a thin wood of Scotch fir and larch is in keeping with our knowledge that it forms an association with these trees called mycorrhiza (fungus root), of mutual benefit to the fungus and tree.

110

The Spike Cap (*Gomphidius glutinosus*) Beatrix already knew well (see page 87). In August 1895 at Holehird she painted two other Spike Caps. The Pine Spike Cap (*Gomphidius viscidus*, now identified as *Chroogomphus rutilus*) is associated with pines. This is almost a purely technical portrait (111) with its long

sections of stems. On 7 August Beatrix painted another species now identified as *Chroogomphus maculatus* (112) showing an attractive group of fungi among grass and, on the same sheet, all the botanical detail. This species is found among larch trees.

112

111

SUMMER 1896

In the summer of 1896 Beatrix was once again in the Lake District, at Sawrey, Ambleside. Her journal for this holiday contains many references to fungi. The letter was written on 20 August 1896.

Lakefield
Sawrey
Ambleside

Do you think this is B[*oletus*] versipellis? I got it in the same place last year, always bright chesnut [sic] colour and rather velvety when first gathered. B. scaber does not grow at all freely here, and I think rather different to Dunkeld, generally hard shiny and wrinkled. I should be glad of any *pezizas*. Mr Massee at Kew Gardens can name them from dried specimens. He says they have been drawn less than agarics and advised me to keep to one division of fungi. I find plenty of microscopic pezizas but no large ones yet and I should be very much obliged if you could send me any, especially any larger ones, which grow on the ground. The young specs [specimens] of B. versipellis (?) have remains of a veil, it is always badly eaten by slugs, grows in gravel at the edge of lake.

113

The *Boletus* Beatrix thought to be *versipellis* has now been identified from her painting (113) made at Windermere in August 1896 as *Leccinum aurantiacum*. There is, however, another painting labelled *Boletus scaber* var. *fulvus* which has now been identified by the experts as the species *versipelle*, with its changing skin colour shown (see page 74). At the end of Beatrix's letter are some words written in Charlie's hand, almost as if he were considering how to reply: 'B. scaber and versipellis are very like. I dare say one would need to see them very often to be able to know the differences easily, but still your specs [specimens] are *versipellis* I doubt not . . .'

114

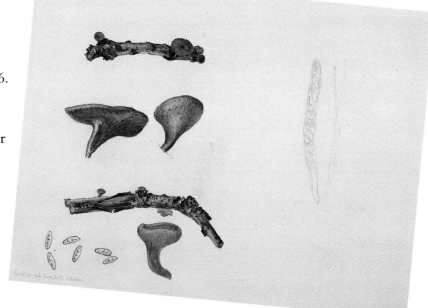

115

114. *Poculum* species,
Lakefield, August 1896.

115. *Poculum firmum*,
Elterholme, September
1896.

'I should be glad of any *pezizas*.' Fungi in the family
Pezizaceae, the Cup Fungi, are quite different from the
toadstools in structure. In toadstools the spores are
formed on tiny club-shaped cells called basidia while Cup
Fungi have their spores in cylindrical or elliptical cases
called asci.

Mr Massee was probably right in telling Beatrix they had been less closely studied than toadstools but she lost no time in taking his advice. There are about thirty beautiful paintings of small Cup Fungi in the Armitt Collection dating from 1896–7. Charlie also took a great interest in this group. During that holiday of 1896, while staying at Lakefield, she made a study on 31 August of one now called *Poculum* (114) on the petioles of oak leaves at Elterholme, on 15 September another (115) now recognised as *Poculum firmum* on what she called 'oak twigs, drift', presumably driftwood by the lake, exactly the habitat of this fungus. The magnified asci, the spore cases, and spores are shown in both these paintings.

116. George Massee

The mention of her conversations with Mr Massee at the Royal Botanic Gardens, Kew, marks a new stage in Beatrix's development as a mycologist. By now she was taking her research very seriously and she had also begun to meet the 'experts' on her own account. This had initially been possible through the good offices of her uncle, Sir Henry Roscoe, at that time Vice-Chancellor of the University of London. Sir Henry was a chemist, not a botanist, but, as a leading figure in the scientific world, he could give Beatrix an introduction to the Director of the Royal Botanic Gardens at Kew, W. T. Thiselton-Dyer, though it appears he was dilatory in actually doing so. On 27 February 1896 Beatrix wrote in her journal, 'Says I, he will give me a note to Mr Thiselton-Dyer' but it wasn't until 19 May that Uncle Harry had a 'a sudden fit of kindness of conscience' and proposed taking her next day to Kew.

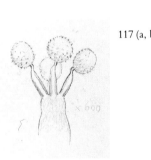

117 (a, b)

117. Microscope drawings by Beatrix of a basidium of a Gill Fungus (a) and an ascus of a Cup Fungus (b).

118. The Reverend John
Stevenson of Glamis.

BEATRIX AND THE EXPERTS

In the 1880s, when Beatrix started painting fungi, the expert mycologists were amateurs like the Reverend M. J. Berkeley and the Reverend John Stevenson of Glamis, whose newly published book Rupert Potter had sent to Charlie in 1887. A hundred years earlier a weaver in Yorkshire, James Bolton, had published one of the first British fungus books, *An History of Fungusses Growing about Halifax*, and in the middle of the nineteenth century Mr and Mrs Hussey had produced *Illustrations of British Mycology*, comprising two sets of beautiful paintings along with scholarly, pithy information about each of several hundred fungi. Mrs Hussey remarked that 'many an eye which is caught by a *flower* does not see a *fungus*.' Nature study, especially botany, became a Victorian craze and Field Clubs flourished all over the country.

The Perthshire Society for Natural Sciences was set up in Perth in 1867 and the Cryptogamic Society of Scotland was also founded there at a great Fungus Show and dinner in 1875. The guest of honour and principal speaker on that occasion was Dr M. C. Cooke, another part-time mycologist but one whose aim was to bring botany to the people. In 1862 he published a delightful little volume, *A Plain and Easy Account of British Fungi*, well illustrated in colour. In 1866 he was co-founder and editor of the journal *Science Gossip*, 'An Illustrated Medium of Interchange and Gossip for Students and LOVERS OF NATURE' (*sic*). The Armitt sisters subscribed and contributed to *Science Gossip*. Cooke also founded the club devoted to microscopy, the Queckett Microscopical Club, which by the time of the Perth dinner in 1875 had no fewer than 600 members, all, of course, men.

In 1880, after a great deal of procrastination by the authorities, Cooke was appointed as cryptogamic botanist at the Royal Botanic Gardens at Kew under Sir Joseph D. Hooker, although only on a part-time basis. He stayed there until 1892 when, to use Cooke's own words, he was banished from Kew by the then Director, W. T. Thiselton-Dyer. According to a contemporary botanist, Thiselton-Dyer was 'a very exalted and unapproachable person' and 'actcd as though he was the owner of the place [Kew] rather than its custodian'. He had married Hooker's daughter, hyphenated his name in 1891 and was knighted in 1899.

By 1896, when Beatrix first went to Kew, a protégé of Cooke, George Massee, had succeeded him but on a full-time basis. He came from Yorkshire, cradle of many fine mycologists. He was a founder member of the British Mycological Society and its first president in 1896 but within a few years he had quarrelled with the office-bearers so violently that he resigned. As a consequence he was rather cut off from other mycologists who were beginning to experiment with fungi. His publications were assessed by them as 'a mixture of sound fact and carelessness'. Even in print he made stupid mistakes, recording spore measurements in whole inches instead of parts of a millimetre. Charlie McIntosh carefully corrected at least one such silly mistake in his copy of *British Fungi*. It is noticeable that neither Massee nor Thiselton-Dyer recommended Cooke's publications, which would have helped Beatrix very much, and one can only think it must have been because his name was unmentionable at Kew!

This, then, was the hornet's nest into which Beatrix and her uncle, Sir Henry Roscoe, stepped. The occasion of her first visit to Kew on 20 May 1896 is recorded in her journal. 'I only hope I shall remember separately the five different gentlemen with whom I had the honour of shaking hands.'

These five men included Mr Massee, 'a very pleasant, kind gentleman who seemed to like my drawings', Mr Baker, the librarian, who had 'an appearance of having been dried in blotting paper under a press', and Mr Thiselton-Dyer, 'a thin, elderly gentleman in summery attire, with a dry, cynical manner, puffing a cigarette but wide awake and boastful. He seemed pleased with my

119

119. William Thiselton-Dyer.

drawings and a little surprised. He spoke kindly about the ticket, and did not address me again, which I mention not with resentment, for I was getting dreadfully tired, but I had once or twice an amusing feeling of being regarded as young.'

The gardens at Kew were not at that time open to visitors but were reserved for scientific study by botanists and a few privileged members of the public who were issued with special tickets. Thiselton-Dyer apparently authorised a ticket for Beatrix and a month later, on 13 June, she returned to Kew alone.

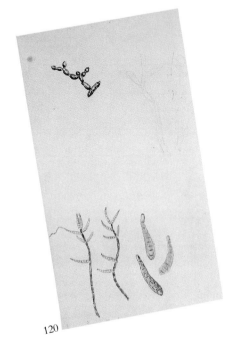

> I went to Kew again to see Mr Massee. I was not a little amused – I hope not disrespectfully. He seems a kind, pleasant gentleman. I believe it is rather the fashion to make fun of him, but I can only remark that it is much more interesting to talk to a person with ideas, even if they are not founded on very sufficient evidence.
>
> He was growing funguses in little glass covers, and, being carried away, confided that one of them had spores three inches long. I opine that he has passed several stages of development into a fungus himself – I am occasionally conscious of a similar transformation . . .

120

121

121. Beatrix took the opportunity during this visit to Kew to pick a Glistening Ink Cap fungus, *Coprinus micaceus*, which she took home and painted. The picture is marked 'Kew, 13 June '96'.

120. The micro-fungus, *Helminthosporium*, on grass (above right), also came from one of Beatrix's visits to Kew; it is marked 'Kew, June 26th 96'. An unidentified contaminant can be seen at the top of the picture.

These episodes show that, far from being overawed by the authorities, Beatrix was becoming more and more confident about her own judgement. During her 1896 summer holiday in the Lake District when she wrote the letter to Charlie about Pezizas we know from her journal that she was thinking hard about theories of fungal reproduction and how spores grew. On 31 August she wrote: 'had further ideas about fungi . . . (I have much pleasure in contradicting Mr G. Murray re. Ascobolus; whether I grow it or not I stick to it.)'

Mr Murray was the keeper of Botany at the Natural History Museum, another 'expert' for whom Beatrix did not have the greatest respect.

Once Beatrix returned to London in November she continued her investigations into the physiology of the gill fungi, especially how they reproduced from spores as well as mycelium, and her experiments in growing spores herself were so successful that, with Uncle Harry's encouragement, she decided to submit her work to Kew. Both she and her uncle foresaw the difficulties likely to be encountered by an amateur.

> [Uncle Harry] invented a fishing letter to Mr Massee at Kew to ask for the name of a book, by way of finding out what they knew, without saying what I did. He was not sanguine, 'you have to discover a great deal that has been done before, before you find anything new'.

And indeed, in reply to this letter, all Beatrix got was the recommendation to read the many volumes by the German authority Brefeld, who was a pioneer in the culture of spores. Did Massee imagine Beatrix could not read German and that this would keep her quiet? He would not have expected her to dismiss the great authority as 'discursive and unstable as – as *Dacrymyces*'. This is a splendid mycological insult as *Dacrymyces* is a 'jelly' fungus. Uncle Harry was as well read in German as in English having been a student at Heidelberg under Bunsen (of Bunsen burner fame).

DREAM OF TOASTED CHEESE

NH_3

"The peculiar pungent smell of this compound is noticed if we heat a bit of **CHEESE** in a test-tube."
Roscoe and Lant.

HBP De 99

122

The very next day Beatrix drove over to Kew in the pony trap 'in a state of damp resignation' but 'discovered in two minutes that Mr Massee knew very little about it.' He seems not to have believed that Beatrix had successfully germinated spores in spite of the evidence of her drawings. The meeting was unsatisfactorily inconclusive.

During November 1896 Beatrix had her work properly typed out. She wrote to Thiselton-Dyer, 'We wish very much that someone would take it up at Kew to try it, if they do not believe my drawings. Mr Massee took objection to my slides, but the things exist.' On 3 December she went to Kew, intending to deliver her paper in person to Thiselton-Dyer, but, on her own admission, she was 'seized with shyness' and 'bolted' without seeing him.

By 7 December, however, she had plucked up courage to go again. There is this delightful account in the journal of her encounter with Thiselton-Dyer:

> Very dree he was, and in a great hurry. I was not shy, not at all. I had it up and down with him. His line was on the outside edge of civil, but I took it philosophically as a compliment to my appearance: he indicated that the subject was profound, that my 'opinions . . .' etc., 'mares' nests . . .' etc., that he hadn't time to look at my drawings, and referred me to the University of Cambridge. I informed him that it would all be in the books in ten years, whether or no, and departed giggling. I ought to wear blue spectacles on these occasions.

Thiselton-Dyer sent an indignant letter about the visit to Beatrix's uncle Harry which he refused to let her see. ('I imagine it contained advice that I should be sent to school before I began to teach other people.') Beatrix shrewdly guessed that Thiselton-Dyer was a 'short-tempered, clever man with a very good opinion of his Establishment, and jealous of outsiders. I am sure I should have been glad to make over my knowledge, and,

122. 'A Dream of Toasted Cheese', 1899 (from a private collection). Beatrix presented this to her Uncle Harry in honour of his textbook, *First Step in Chemistry*. The Bunsen burner was a recent invention of Uncle Harry's former mentor at Heidelberg.

being a student there, I should think they might have taken it over without derogation.' However, the rift proved advantageous to Beatrix. 'It was the very luckiest thing that could have happened, for Uncle Harry was just sufficiently annoyed at the slighting of anything under his patronage to make him take it up all the harder,' and with Uncle Harry's help she began to prepare a formal paper for presentation to the Linnean Society.

Meanwhile Mr Massee at Kew had also 'come round altogether' and was at last prepared to believe that Beatrix had succeeded in her experiments to germinate spores. When she visited Kew she had found him 'making efforts to grow *Bulgaria inquinans* [the Black Bulgar] quite ineffectually'. After Thiselton-Dyer's rude response she sent Massee two of her own slips of *Bulgaria inquinans*. (She hoped 'he may show them to the Director'.) We have a sheet of Beatrix's drawings of the spores of this fungus dated August 1895. Beatrix also notes in her journal that on this visit she gave Massee 'a slice of *velutipes*, highly poisoned'! Did she really expect him to try to grow it?

123

124

Bulgaria inquinans is a Cup Fungus related to Peziza.

When she went back to Kew early in January 1897, however, she found that Massee had grown one of her 'best moulds' and although she did not suspect him of 'any design of poaching' she was aware of the dangers of having her ideas taken over without acknowledgement.

What Beatrix called 'moulds' (one of them is *Penicillium*) are quite easy to grow in artificial culture; in fact they grow only too well and so contaminated many of Beatrix's cultures. The spores of the gill fungi, the Agaricineae, the old-fashioned term used in the title of her paper for mushrooms and toadstools, are much more difficult. This was what Beatrix's drawings definitely show she succeeded in doing.

BEATRIX'S SCIENTIFIC PAPER

Over Christmas and the New Year of 1897 Beatrix's journal shows how seriously she was working on her paper.

> Saturday, December 26th – Having worked very hard till twelve last night . . . was kept all morning, Uncle Harry going over and over it with a pencil. It will want a great deal more work in references and putting together, but no matter.

The next letter from Beatrix to Charlie was written on 12 January 1897, just when the preparations were at their height.

> 2 Bolton Gardens
> London S.W.
> Jan 12th 97

Do you think you could get me a fungus called corticium amorphum? It grows on fir bark and looks at first like Lachnea calycina, but afterwards sticky like Dacrymyces.

　Also I should be very much obliged if you could give me any information about Merulius corium. You told me some time since that you had not found it at Dunkeld with properly developed spore[s]. Do you mean every season, or only in unfavourable seasons? Have you noticed the same thing with any other fungus? For instance Chlorosplenium aeruginosum? I am doing some curious work with fungus spore; trying to draw up a paper with the assistance of my uncle Sir H. Roscoe. Have you ever suspected that there are *intermediate* species amongst Agarics and Boleti? We are strongly of opinion for certain good reasons that there are mixed fungi – that is to say – either growing actually upon a mixed network of mycelium, or else hybrid species which have originated in that way. I do not express any opinion which way, only that they *are* intermediate.

Of course such an idea is contrary to the books, except for lichens, but I should be curious to hear *whether you have had difficulty in naming any of the sorts* which I suspect. Have you noticed whether fungi described as 'varieties' are constant in type? For instance, does A[*garicus*] aureus var. vahlii, come up the same every season? And *all* the season? I mean to say are there poor specimens towards the end of the season more like the ordinary A. aureus? I do not mean to suggest the idea if you have not noticed it yourself. (It may be a different species, not a var. at all.) I have found a fungus very like A. velutipes which Sir Henry thinks is either a mixture or a new sort. There is no harm in giving an opinion, so long as it is made clear whether it is only an opinion, or the result of observation; we find some people make theories out of dried specimens without the least experience of the way things grow. If you find Corticium would you please wrap it up as soon as found, to keep the spore separate. If you take any interest in physiology I should be amused to send a copy later on. We have got into contradictions at Kew and British Museum already, but I think my uncle is a good judge. Do you know anything about lichens?

Beatrix Potter

Beatrix begins this letter with an excellent description of a fungus she would like to have, *Corticium amorphum (amorphum* = without form, shapeless). Stevenson was particularly interested in this strange little fungus which he found on silver firs around Dunkeld and Perth. It is only 2 or 3 cm across, tinged orange in colour, at first cup shaped and then flattened. In Europe some authorities thought it was a true Cup Fungus, a *Peziza*, even after examining it under the microscope. In Beatrix's time it was scarcely known in England, almost all the reports coming from Scotland where Stevenson was considering whether it should be transferred to a new genus. In fact in

1888 this had been done in Germany and *Corticium amorphum* became *Aleurodiscus amorphus,* which is how it is still classified today.

There is a sheet of Beatrix's drawings which we now know shows *Aleurodiscus amorphus.* However, it has no name on it, only the words, written very faintly in pencil, 'lichen on fir, Dunkeld'. We can only speculate whether Charlie had sent her this earlier as a lichen – there are lichens on silver firs that look very like *Aleurodiscus* but it is unlikely he would have made this mistake.

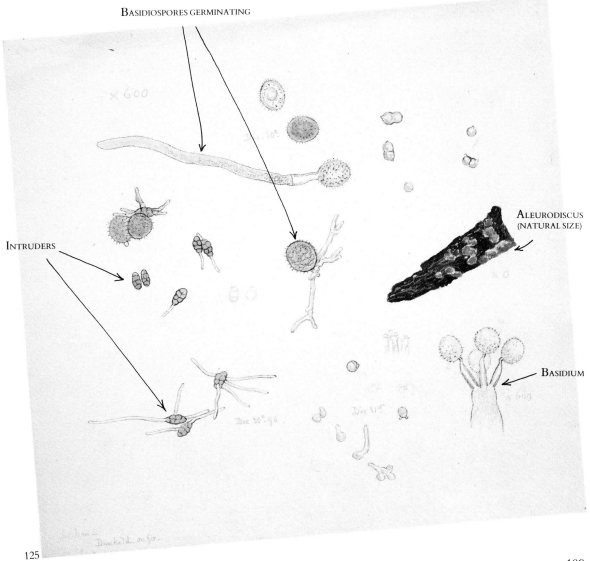

BASIDIOSPORES GERMINATING

INTRUDERS

ALEURODISCUS
(NATURAL SIZE)

BASIDIUM

125

On 30 December 1896 Beatrix, according to her journal, took a 'lichen, grown' to the Natural History Museum to ask Mr Murray, Keeper of Botany, about it. ('I did not expect that he would know but I wanted to hear what he would say.') Murray dismissed it as 'not a lichen' but a fungus called *Naematelia*. She seems to have shown Mr Murray drawings as well as the specimen.

In 1961 '*Naematelia*' was found to have been based on two fungi, not one as required by the Rules of Botanical Nomenclature, and so the name was abolished. One of the fungi comprising *Naematelia* was a Jelly Fungus, a *Tremella*, and at least one species of *Tremella* has been found to be a parasite on *Aleurodiscus amorphus*! It would seem likely therefore that the sheet of drawings reproduced on the previous page was the one actually shown to Mr Murray. It was confidently identified in 1986 as *Aleurodiscus amorphus* by Dr Watling, who commented that Stevenson's description of the fungus could have been taken from this sheet, they agree so well.

There is no evidence that Beatrix herself ever recognised it as the *Corticium amorphum* she asked Charlie to send.

'I am doing some curious work with fungus spore . . . We find some people make theories out of dried specimens without the least experience of the way things

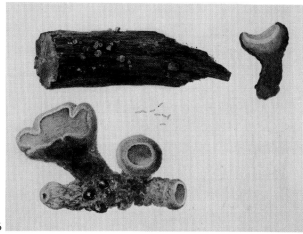

126. *Chlorosplenium*, now *Chlorociboria aeruginascens*, which Beatrix mentions in this letter, is interesting as wood infected with it turns green. This characterises the old genuine 'Tunbridge Ware', small hand-crafted objects made in the town of Tunbridge Wells in Kent. The green stain in the wood can be seen at the top left of the picture.

126

grow.' What a heartfelt indictment of the professionals in London with whom Beatrix and her uncle had indeed 'got into contradictions'.

'Do you know anything about lichens?' It was with Mr George Murray at the Natural History Museum that the contradictions about lichens arose. Beatrix reports in her journal how, following their conversation about 'Naematelia', she was able to embarrass him with a series of questions on lichens. 'I asked . . . his views on the Schwendener theory. I asked him whether the algae had spores too, or how it came to be always to hand.' The German authority Schwendener was the first to report that a lichen was a dual organism, a compound plant consisting of a fungus growing in close association with an alga. This basic idea is now accepted as correct, but the experts are still debating Beatrix's precise question about their relationship; are they mutually beneficial or is one parasitising the other? The other point she raised was how it happened that the alga and fungus came together, how the spores 'came to be always to hand'. We now know an answer to that one; at least some lichens make up little dispersal packages in which the alga is enmeshed in the fungal threads so the two partners travel together. It is little wonder, however, that, faced with these searching questions, Mr Murray 'fled and so did Miss Smith, the librarian'. This lady was very probably Miss Annie Lorraine Smith who became a great authority on lichens and in 1905 one of the first lady members of the Linnean Society.

GREY LICHEN

JELLY FUNGUS

127. This painting shows grey lichen and a yellow jelly fungus or Myxomycetes on a twig, with the yellow organism shown much enlarged below.

127

In 1897 Charlie, like Beatrix, was preparing a paper for a learned society. His was for the Perthshire Society of Natural Science and was on the subject of larch disease as he knew it in Dunkeld.[1] The next letter from Beatrix, following only ten days after the last, is in reply to one from Charlie which apparently included an account of his observations.

Five of the very first larch trees from Europe, *Larix europea*, were planted in 1738 near the cathedral at Dunkeld. One still stands. Soon, however, they were attacked by a disease, 'canker', which became so serious that it was the subject of much study on the continent as well as in Scotland. Charlie's paper is a classic account of the ecology of the disease, where aphids apparently caused great exudation of resin around the canker and even resulted in the increase in the numbers of birds, especially the 'Tit kind'. Great, Coal, Blue and Long-tailed Tits as well as Goldcrests became more numerous as they fed on the aphids. But Charlie also noted on the cankered 'swollen, blistered parts' a very small Cup Fungus belonging to the same family as *Peziza* and now called *Lachnellula willkommii*. 'Whether it is the fungus or the aphis, or both in conjunction, that causes the destruction is a question which I cannot answer,' though Charlie quotes the German authority Tubeuf who thought the fungus merely grew on wounds and was not the primary parasite.

How many of all these interesting observations were in the letter Beatrix referred to we can only guess. This is her reply:

> Jan 22nd, 97
> 2, Bolton Gardens
> London, S.W.
>
> Thank you very much for your interesting letter, especially about the larch disease. I have taken note

---

[1] *Notes by a Naturalist round Dunkeld* by C. McIntosh, Inver, read 10 February 1898, published in the Transactions of the Society.

of it in the Lake District but never saw any aphis, but of course it is a disadvantage not to be able to examine the trees at different seasons. I should think if a tree is weakened by one parasite it is less able to withstand the attack of another; or possibly the peziza spore may get into the larch through the blister and bleeding caused by the aphis. The peziza mycelium is very vigorous and spreads in the red lower layer of bark. I have seen it come out in that layer on a broken dead branch at several inches from the fungus. I quite came to the same conclusion about the bleeding of resin – that it is the peculiar constitution of the larch which does the mischief; I think the fungus does not penetrate at all deeply but that the scar, being open, eats into the trunk. It is so bad in Westmorland that one does not find one straight stem in 500. The woodmen think it is caused by replanting without cleaning up, and if the fungus *is* the cause they are right to some extent, because it breeds to an extraordinary extent on heaps of sticks. There is something odd about that particular fungus, supposing it is the cause of the disease, for others very like it seem harmless. I have seen one very like it in Gloucestershire and Surrey but the live trees were scarcely diseased at all.

I think I have found the new fungus again. I can hardly describe the difference; it is drier than velutipes both pileus and gills, rather broader and shorter and a peculiar smell, gills a deep yellow when old, also inclined to become discoloured in patches.

My difficulty about lichens is to find ripe spore for experiments. I scarcely know what to look for. I have succeeded in growing spore of Cladonia, but *larger* spores would be more convenient. You see we do not believe in Schwendener's theory, and the older books say that the lichens pass gradually into hepaticas through the foliaceous species. I should like very much to grow the spore of one of those

128. Pixie Cup (*Cladonia pyxidata*).

128

large flat lichens, and also the spore of a real *hepatica* in order to compare the 2 ways of sprouting. The names do not matter as I can dry them. If you could get me any spore of the lichen and hepatica when the weather changes I should be very much obliged.

With regard to the drawings I have no objection at all, but wish that they were better worth lending. I think you have one of S. strobilaceous which is a curiosity. The fungologist at Kew said he had only seen it once – in the summer of 95 – when he found any quantity in a wood near Watford, Hertfordshire.

I remain yours sincerely
Beatrix Potter

Beatrix and Charlie certainly between them came to the right conclusion about the cause of the larch canker, a conclusion confirmed by the experts many years later. The primary cause is a Cup Fungus, *Peziza*, now named

129. *Lachnellula* species on bark.

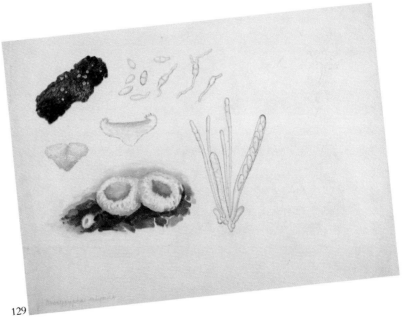

129

Lachnellula willkommii, but another one, closely related and very like it, follows it into the damaged tissues. This is *Lachnellula occidentalis*. When Beatrix was at Sawrey in July 1896 she collected material of 'larch canker' and made some fine composite paintings.

130. Until very recently this sheet was taken to represent only the causal fungus, *Lachnellula willkommii*, but close expert examination has enabled us to conclude that *both* fungi are depicted. The twig in the top right corner has on it the species *L. occidentalis*, and under it the cankered, swollen twig has *L. willkommii*. Whether Beatrix was aware of this we now have no means of knowing. Yet another small 'intruder' fungus has been included in the bottom left-hand corner of the sheet, a *Nectria*.

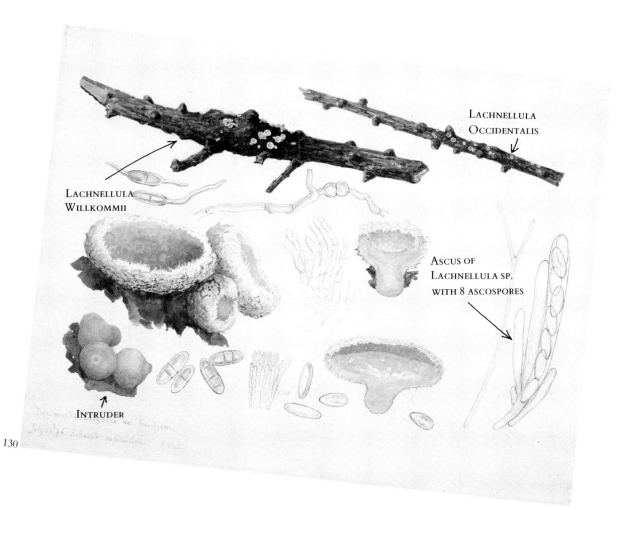

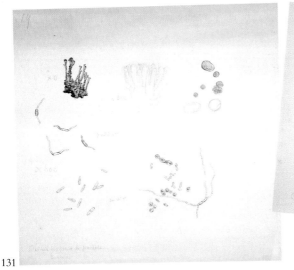

131

132

133

134

135

131. *Cladonia* is one of the group of 'Reindeer' lichens, named thus because they are an important part of the diet of reindeer. As Beatrix wrote, they are not flat but erect. The species *pyxidata*, which is shown here and on page 113, is well known as the Pixie Cup, the little red top being the fruit of the fungus partner. The two detailed drawings of the *Cladonia* spore germinating show (132) the spore of the alga partner and (133) the spore of the fungus partner.

134. In almost all British lichens, as in *Cladonia*, the fungal part belongs to the class ascomycetes, the Cup Fungi, described on page 98. The only notable exceptions include some basidiomycetes, Gill Fungi, of the genus *Omphalina* found characteristically among mosses and heathers in damp, peaty places. *Omphalina pseudoandrosacea*, which Beatrix painted at Eastwood in 1893, is a lichen-former; but this is a recent discovery that neither Beatrix nor Charlie could know about. The name *Omphalina* comes from the Latin *omphalos*, the navel, referring to the little depression on the cap.

135. Beatrix made a very accurate drawing of this flat lichen, a species of *Stereocaulon*.

'The older books say that the lichens pass gradually into hepatics . . .' These must have been very old books as it had been shown in Germany in 1784 that this was wrong.

Beatrix's mention of the fact that she had no objection at all to her drawings being shown may give a clue as to how they came to be in the Museum at Perth. Charlie, as an Associate of the Perthshire Society for Natural Science, often sent material for exhibition. It is quite probable, therefore, that the first exhibition of Beatrix Potter's paintings of fungi was at Perth or Dunkeld about 1897. If so the Old Man of the Woods, *Strobilomyces floccopus*, would certainly have been included (see page 72).

A month later Beatrix wrote again to Charlie.

> Feb 22nd 97
> 2, Bolton Gardens
> S.W.

I am very much obliged to you for the 2 parcels, the hepatica is particularly curious. I hope very much I shall succeed in getting the spore to sprout. I have had a good deal of trouble about the paper. I am afraid the best part of my work will have to stand over till next season. The thing which causes so much contradiction is that I succeeded in sprouting the mushroom spore, which I supposed is what it is meant for; but it seems that no one else is admitted to have done it, and therefore no one except my uncle and one gentleman at Kew will believe that any of my slides are right. I have grown between 40 and 50 sorts of spore, but I think we shall probably only send in A. velutipes, which I have grown twice and Mr Massee has also grown according to my direction at Kew. He did not previously believe in the things at all. I am just as much sure of the mushroom but unless I can get a good slide actually sprouting it seems useless to send it to the Linnaean. I should be obliged if you would *not* mention it to anyone concerned with botany, until the paper is really sent, because without meaning to be uncivil they are more inclined to grow the things themselves than to admit that mine are right. What I have been doing is to sort out the 'Hyphomycetes' which in great part are not real 'species' at all, which has been suspected for a long time, but it was not previously known that they belonged to Agarics as well as to pezizas. Please do not send anything more just now because my slides are full of mushrooms; which refuse to grow when required.

Beatrix Potter

So Charlie sent the hepatic, the liverwort, as requested. Would that the experts in London had been so helpful! Beatrix's exasperation with them is very clear in her journal for December 1896 and January 1897.

> I was afraid the Director would have taken away my ticket. I fancy he may be something of a misogynist . . . but it is odious to a shy person to be snubbed as conceited, especially when the shy person happened to be right.

It is tantalising that Beatrix Potter's journal finishes without explanation on 31 January 1897, just when her work with the fungi and the lichens was coming to a climax, so we have no further information here on the 'trouble about the paper'.

She certainly succeeded in drawing the spores of many fungi in the process of germinating, but a number show that contaminants, unwanted 'moulds' like *Penicillium* invaded her slides. Some, however, notably the sheet of *Aleurodiscus* already described on page 109, show that she was absolutely right – she had succeeded where so many had failed or not even tried. What perhaps Beatrix did not realise was that the spores she was working with, the basidiospores of the agarics, are much more difficult to grow artificially than others. In America, for instance, commercial mushroom growers at the time of Beatrix's work were importing their 'spawn', the mycelium, from

France. When they decided to grow it for themselves they discovered just how difficult that was. Eventually a paper was published in 1902 claiming success, followed by definitive work in 1928 – all this with complete laboratory facilities which Beatrix did not have.

136. Beatrix painted one of the common hepatics, or liverworts, *Marchantia*. The 'breathing pores' are shown, these corresponding to stomata in green plants. A painting of a leafy liverwort, *Porella laevigata*, is shown on page 129. Beatrix mistook it for a moss.

136

There is a long gap of seven months until the last letter in the Dunkeld collection. This was probably written from the Lake District, from Lingholm, Keswick, and is dated 21 September 1897. The visitors' book at Kew shows that Beatrix had been there several times in the spring of 1897, and during the summer she was still painting and identifying fungi.

Sept. 21st 97

I was very much pleased with the beautiful specimens of A[*garicus*] lenticularis. I never saw the Boletus before I think. I can very likely get the same at Kew, it was peculiar in having a very hard edge. The Boletuses here seem to be most of them neither one thing nor another. I have found a good many I could not name but there are none worth sending just now. I have put in a few seeds of the wild balsam, it is not uncommon at the Lakes, growing 3 foot high in damp places, such as ditches under trees. I am afraid the flowers may not be worth much after packing. The fungus is one of a large clump on a stump. I have got a good photograph of it so I wish I could name it; it is not smooth *at first*. I am not sure if you sent it to me once. I found the Hygrophorus before, at Coldstream.

I am trying to work out the moulds – conidial forms – of the mushrooms; exceedingly difficult to grow. My paper was read at the Linnaean Society, and 'well received' according to Mr Massee, but they say it requires more work in it before it is printed.

I find no difficulty in sprouting the mycelium of any fungus, but the 'spawn' is so very difficult to run. If I am right it will be possible to work out which of the Boleti are hybrids, but it will take many years at the present rate! Your Boletus was a little too stale to sprout, and A. lenticularis I am afraid is not starting; Lactarius seems to be easy.

[It appears that this letter is incomplete.]

137. *Agaricus lenticularis* (now *Limacella guttata*) has dewlike droplets at the edge of the gills, thought to look like lentils, hence the old specific name. It was an old friend of both Charlie and Beatrix; she painted it in Dunkeld in October 1893, having found it at the Hermitage, a lovely woodland near Inver now in the care of the National Trust for Scotland.

It is not at all surprising that Beatrix found the Boletuses 'neither one thing nor another', as already discussed. Wild Balsam, or Touch-me-not (*Impatiens noli-tangere*), gets its name from the way the ripe seeds shoot out from the plants when touched. Beatrix noted the lovely 'milky lemon-blue' colour of the seeds and knew this plant, common in the Lake District but not found around Dunkeld, would interest Charlie. The *Hygrophorus* she had found at Coldstream could be the 'lovely pink one', *calyptraeformis*, with the hood (see page 85).

137

138

Beatrix had indeed succeeded in getting the spawn 'to run' with the hairy bracket fungus, *Stereum hirsutum* (139), as the microscope drawings below show. The little bumps in the mycelium are now known to mycologists as clamp connections. They are characteristic of the hyphae, or 'spawn' of such fungi. It is extremely unlikely that Beatrix knew about them when she faithfully drew them but they are certainly proof that the spawn was growing.

139

140

141

The details of the fate of her paper are not known. In the Proceedings of the Linnean Society of London it is recorded that a paper 'On the Germination of the Spores of *Agaricineae*' by Miss Helen B. Potter was read on 1 April 1897. Being a woman, Beatrix could not present this in person or attend on the occasion. George Massee undertook to read the paper on her behalf but the main speaker on that day was Thiselton-Dyer. We cannot tell whether Beatrix's drawings were ever seen by the members and there is now no trace of the paper in the Linnean. She may even have destroyed it herself, although her journal entry about her uncle Harry 'going over and over it with a pencil' includes the statement, 'I shall keep those pencil marks when I am an old woman.'

The dismissal of her paper by the Linnean Society must have been a considerable disappointment to her in spite of Massee's attempt to soften the blow. But we know her interest in mycology was not quite suppressed, and she continued to study and paint fungi for several years after the publication of *The Tale of Peter Rabbit* had changed her life.

Charles McIntosh had expert help from such as Dr F. Buchanan White, Reverend John Stevenson and even Reverend M. J. Berkeley. Beatrix Potter had no similar support; even Uncle Harry, a truly eminent scientist, was a chemist, not a biologist, and George Massee did not have a 'completely clear head'. Only Charlie gave her the guidance she needed. After his death she wrote:

> He was a keen observer and first-rate field naturalist fifty years ago, and the kind of student who would continue to learn throughout a long life. It is very fitting that his name and example should be remembered and honoured in his native place. The only lasting peacefulness is Nature, and it would be well if children – old and young – would study it like Charlie McIntosh.

MOSSES

Among the Dunkeld letters about fungi is an undated note from Beatrix to Charlie which relates to mosses. It was probably written fairly early in their correspondence when Charlie was sending batches of fungi for Beatrix to paint. In her letter of 10 December 1892 (page 66) she wrote, 'The moss is more trouble on account of being magnified, and Miss Potter thinks she will keep any drawings of moss, to add to her set.' We now have twenty-eight exquisite paintings of mosses. As in the painting of *Dicranella* (opposite) there is a little sketch of the moss at about natural size while important parts such as fruits (capsules) and leaf tips are 'magnified' about ten or twelve times as seen under a strong hand-lens. We have no idea where the paintings were done but around Dunkeld and in the Lake District there are many rather special mosses. Both mosses and ferns were of great interest to Charlie.

This is the note.

> I find I have a drawing of Dicranella heteromalla, and unfinished drawings of P. undulatum and P. aloides. I am much obliged to you for writing the list of names with reference to 'Stark' which I begin to understand at last. I have looked at all the mosses carefully and drawn some of the larger varieties. I suppose the fruit of H. splendens is very uncommon. I have never found any, nor on H. proliferum or H. molluscum. I made quite a large picture of the fine fungus which you sent before Christmas. I hope to show it to you some time.

The 'Stark' she refers to is a delightful little book written by Robert M. Stark in 1854, *A Popular History of British Mosses*. He was a dealer in dried specimens of all kinds of plants in business in Princes Street, Edinburgh. Very probably Charlie recommended the book.

As with the fungi, some of the mosses have changed

their names since Beatrix painted them; both names are given below. A few specimens were, however, wrongly identified by Beatrix but her detailed painting is so good that experts can now provide the correct names. Her moss pictures have never been reproduced for publication until this time.

142. *Dicranella heteromalla* is correctly identified and the name is still valid. It is common on acid soils, on heathland.

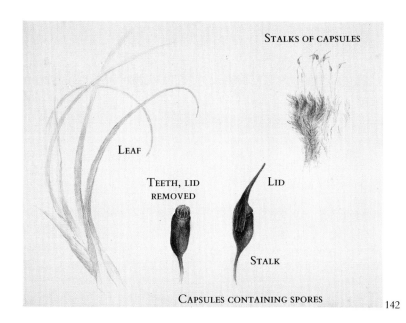

STALKS OF CAPSULES

LEAF

TEETH, LID REMOVED

LID

STALK

CAPSULES CONTAINING SPORES

142

143. *Polytrichum undulatum* (now called *Atrichum undulatum*) is a fine moss, at its best in northern and western Britain. The leaf is undulate or wavy.

143

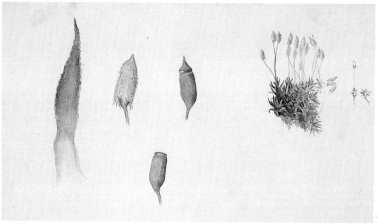

144

144. Beatrix identified this moss as
Polytrichum aloides, the specific name
coming from its resemblance to an aloe
plant. However, it is now in the genus
Pogonatum and the long pointed leaf tip
allows the expert to identify it as another
species closely related to *aloides,
urnigerum*, so the correct name is
Pogonatum urnigerum. It is a moss of
mountain country.

145. It seems from her letter that
Beatrix thought this was *Hylocomium
splendens* but it is now identified as
Pseudoscleropodium purum, a very
common moss worldwide, often found
on lawns; the fruit is uncommon.

145

146

146. This is a portrait of *Hylocomium splendens* showing its reddish stem and short, curved fruit. It is found in grass and heather in upland woods of north and west Britain.

147. Beatrix called this *Hypnum proliferum* but the moss in this painting is *Thuidium tamariscinum*. It looks like a Tamarisk, a European shrub not found in Britain. (The true *Hypnum proliferum* is now regarded as the same as *Hylocomium splendens*.) Fruit is uncommon, curved and borne on a long red stalk. It is a common, bright green moss on damp ground and rotting logs in woods.

H. molluscum mentioned in Beatrix's note stood for *Hypnum molluscum*, now *Ctenidium molluscum*. We have no painting of it, but *Ptilium crista-castrensis*, on page 129, is closely related.

147

148. This is *Bryum capillare*, one of the most abundant British species with a very wide range of habitat, from wall-tops to mountain ledges. The fruit is on a reddish stalk, sharply turned over at the top.

148

149. *Hypnum myosuroides* (now called *Isothecium myosuroides*) is common and widely distributed. It gets its name from the 'mouse tail' appearance of its shoots which have a bare base and a feathery top.

149

150

150. *Hypnum crista-castrensis* (now called *Ptilium crista-castrensis*) is a striking species, occasionally plentiful under conifers in the north. Beatrix found this at Birnam. Charlie knew it as he put a specimen into the collection he made for the Institute in Birnam. It is still there.

151. Leafy liverworts are often mistaken for mosses. This painting shows the liverwort *Porella laevigata*. It grows on limestone in mountainous districts.

151

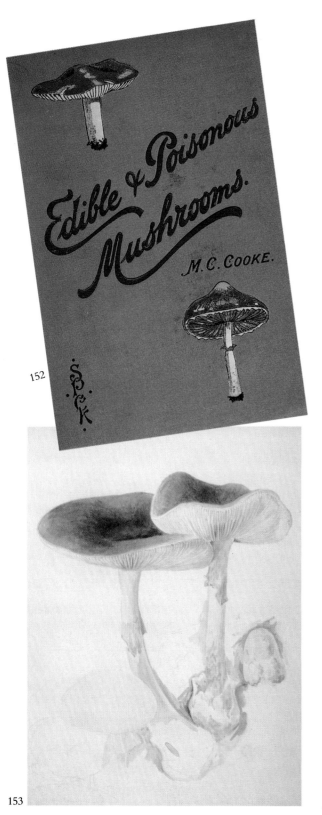

152

153

EDIBLE AND POISONOUS FUNGI

Neither Beatrix nor Charlie were interested in the edibility of fungi, a particularly British attitude in those days, unlike that in Europe. In 1894 M.C. Cooke had published his *Edible and Poisonous Mushrooms*, an attempt to get the British people to eat fungi safely. Louie Armitt had a copy of this book, which is still in the Armitt Collection (shown right). Beatrix certainly knew which species were poisonous, such as the Death Cap (*Amanita phalloides*), below, which she painted at Eastwood, Dunkeld in 1893. This painting is now badly faded.

One of Beatrix's earliest paintings was of the Wood Blewit (see page 61) which was on sale in country markets in England, especially in the Midlands, in her time. On 18 August 1894 she described in her journal the wood at Hatchednize, near Coldstream, as an 'ideal heavenly dream of the toadstool eaters', having found just the day before a first crop of '*Cantharellus cibarius*'. This is the Chanterelle so highly regarded by 'toadstool eaters', especially in Europe (see page 61).

Beatrix made an interesting observation about poisonous Roll Rims (*Paxillus*) in her journal on 10 October 1894. 'There is a line in *The Tempest* about the green, sour ringlets . . . There is actual acidity in the spore of the large Paxillus especially, which blue deadens the actual grass blades

153. Death Cap (*Amanita phalloides*), Dunkeld, 1893.

and merely sours the root too, but this requires observation. I see no mystery in the enlarging [fairy] ring myself.'

154. She painted the poisonous Roll Rim (*Paxillus involutus*) from Tomgarrow in August 1895, as a pleasant group of fungi with, on a separate sheet (155), the long section showing the make-up of the stem. The fungus shown to the right of the sections is *Pilobolus*, a dung inhabitor which shoots its head right off to disperse its spores.

154

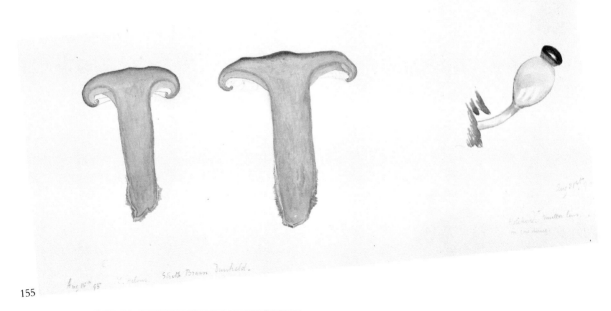

155

156. Deer droppings in Richmond Park provided another specimen of *Pilobolus* sp., dated 13 May 1896. Beatrix was not squeamish about collecting material wherever she could find it.

156

157

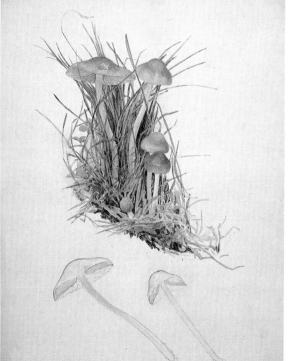

158

157. This is a very good picture of *Paxillus involutus* from Tomgarrow, painted in September 1893.

158. *Marasmius oreades* is the Fairy Ring fungus, shown here in grass. It is toxic to the grass, forming the fairy rings, but can safely be eaten fried. This picture was painted at Coldstream in August 1894.

Many years later, in 1930, in the unpublished sequel to *The Fairy Caravan* we find Cantharella, 'apricot orange coloured and sweet almond smelling . . . she plays about among the beech leaves in September.' Here too appears Boletus with the warning, 'Do not touch him, he is poisonous. Look at his velvet coat, all buff and crimson; but if a bit were broken off his edge it would turn verdigris blue.' This is a very good description of *Boletus erythropus*, poisonous when eaten raw but said to be safe when cooked. It used to be thought that one of the signs of a poisonous fungus, now discredited, was that it turned blue on breaking.

159. The change in colour can be clearly seen in this painting of *Boletus badius* from Smailholm, September 1894.

159

In the earlier adventures of the Fairy Caravan people, poor Paddy Pig became ill through eating toadstool tartlets. He was not only ill but his 'behaviour was odd'. Was this Beatrix popping in the idea of the hallucinogenic effects of a fungus only too well known today as the Magic Mushroom, *Psilocybe semilanceata*, Liberty Cap? The cure for Paddy Pig's illness was the plant known from ancient time as Herb of Grace or Rue, and here again Beatrix drops in a little bit of her scholarship with her reference to the famous Elizabethan herbalist John Gerard whose great *Herball* Mary Ellen consults. 'What says old Gerard in the big calfskin book? . . . Twelve pennyweight of rue is a counter-poison to the poison of wolfs-bane; and mushrooms; and TOADSTOOLS . . .'

We know Beatrix enjoyed eating freshly picked mushrooms. In 1905 when she stayed at Gwaynynog in Wales she wrote to her publisher's daughter, Winifred Warne, describing how she and her cousin went out and picked them. There are sketches of little mushrooms alongside the text which also includes the statement, 'I am going to put a picture of mushrooms in a book!'

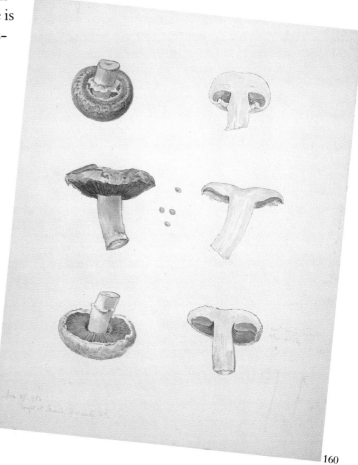

160. On the back of this 1898 study of the Common Field Mushroom (*Agaricus campestris*) Beatrix has written, 'Large basketful, all small, very even in type. Nasty smell but good flavour.'

160

161

162

161, 162. These paintings show the
brown form of the edible, commercial
mushroom, *Agaricus bisporus*. They were
bought in London at 'Slaters' and
painted by Beatrix before being passed
on to the kitchen.

A BOTANICAL FOSSIL
by Mary Noble

Fossils, as well as fungi, were of interest to Beatrix. Summing up her holiday at Lennel, Coldstream, in 1894, she wrote in her journal of 10 October, 'This last morning . . . having finished packing up my fossils in a little box, I went down to the river [Tweed] and proceeded to get more . . .. The funguses will come up again and the fossils will keep. I hope I may go back again some day when I am an old woman, unless I become a fossil myself, which would save trouble.' She then adds, 'I made about forty careful drawings of funguses, and collected some interesting fossils, one of which I find labelled at the Museum [very likely Kelso] Araucarioxylon from Lennel Braes, a lucky find since I know nothing about it.' This is the only fossil she specifically names in her journal.

163. Eight fossils, including corals, from the Applethwaite Beds, Troutbeck, August and September 1895. From the National Trust collection.

164. Six fossils from the Applethwaite Beds found at Sour Howes, Troutbeck, August 1895.

164

Araucarioxylon is extremely interesting to botanists. In 1826 some huge fossil trees found in Craigleith quarry, Edinburgh, were thought to be the prototype of the Monkey Puzzle tree, *Araucaria*. Later research disproved this theory and the Craigleith fossil trees were renamed *Pitus*. Some large fragments of *Pitus* from Craigleith are on display at the Royal Botanic Garden in Edinburgh and another tree trunk was sent over 100 years ago to the Natural History Museum, London, where it still remains. In the National Museum of Scotland there is a prepared specimen of *Pitus* showing the botanical detail; it is labelled as coming from 'Lennel Braes'. No one knows how it reached Edinburgh – it could have come from Kelso!

165. Fossil studies, one drawn at Lennel in October 1894: undetermined wood fragments. The dotted lines indicate the planes chosen for illustration.

165

BEATRIX POTTER'S SCIENTIFIC ART
by Anne Stevenson Hobbs

BACKGROUND

'Now of all hopeless things to draw, I should think the very worst is a fine fat fungus.' Beatrix wrote ruefully in 1892, echoing Constable: 'Art is hopeless: it can never compete with nature'. Beatrix Potter's scientific drawings were pictures with a purpose – not painted just 'to please myself'. Everyone drew flowers, but the fungi were her own discovery; they fired her, and fulfilled her need to do something worthwhile.

For three hundred years women as enthusiastic amateurs had been studying the sciences. Beatrix Potter's lack of formal education stood her in good stead ('Thank goodness, my education was neglected and the originality was not rubbed off'), for by the end of the century in major girls' schools science had been supplanted by Latin and Greek. In her mycological studies Beatrix had little help (pages 103, 123). In her art

166. *Coriolus versicolor*, sent to Beatrix from Pau in France by Miss Cameron, her former governess, in March 1898. Another specimen was sent from the Ardennes.

166

Note The italic numbers in brackets in this section refer to the plate numbers of the illustrations.

167

167. Witches' Butter (*Exidia glandulosa*), drawn at Woodcote in March 1896.

too she was almost self-taught, except for some formal training from a Miss Cameron. Congenial and cosmopolitan influences at Woodcote, home of her uncle Sir Henry Roscoe, helped to broaden her horizons. There she drew plants and animals, often in her cousin Dora's gypsy caravan. Uncle Harry, a polymath, was interested in geology; Canon Rawnsley too encouraged her geological and archaeological pursuits. Laura (Lily) Thornely, related to Beatrix through the Roscoes, may have been the first to arouse her interest in fungi and fossils.

Botanical illustration is 'a peculiar art with an almost total subjugation of creativity to the accurate likeness' (Brinsley Burbidge, 1975). Yet the best practitioners have managed to balance the demands of art and science, and to combine accuracy and beauty. A thorough knowledge of the subject is a prerequisite, and an awareness of its essential elements – and so too is an understanding of colours, coupled with perfect coordination of hand and eye. But above all, the artist must feel passionately about the object before him.

By 1800, flower painting had become a required female accomplishment, and a harmless antidote to frivolity. Sketching was proper and universal; watercolours, being small-scale and clean, were especially recommended to young ladies. By mid-century, thanks largely to Ruskin's influence, art was being systematically taught even to women – and often *by* women. Many women became distinguished botanical artists, and some of these women worked as professionals, Thiselton-Dyer's wife among them. It is particularly ironic that her husband should have dismissed Beatrix Potter's work.

Fungus illustration was slower to develop than the illustration of flowering plants, in part because the anatomy of fungi was poorly understood; some of the earliest pictures were done for decorative purposes (Brent Elliott, *The Garden*, September 1991). James Bolton, mycological pioneer, produced remarkable delicately-coloured etchings for *An History of Fungusses Growing about Halifax* (1788–91). Outstanding in mid-century was the rare *Fungi Hypogaei* of the Brothers Tulasne (1851, on the botany of truffles), and their *Selecta Fungorum Carpologia* (1862–65), with lithographs 'that have never been surpassed in their depiction of microscopic structure of fungi' (Elliott); it was translated into English as late as 1931. Sowerby's *Coloured figures of English fungi or mushrooms* (1797–1803) had been the only attempt to record all the fungi of the British Isles. Later nineteenth-century artists drew mainly from dried specimens, as their work betrays. Cooke was by far the most prolific, and his illustrations have more charm than Massee's (pages 100–1). He hints at texture and habitat, and like Beatrix Potter draws the sections a step behind. The general impression at this period, however, is one of flatness, with colours either crude or pallid (printing methods presented technical problems), and of stiff, static figures in rudimentary settings, with little attention paid to layout.

Well-known artists like Birket Foster and Frederick Walker (admired by Beatrix) saw the fascination in fungi, as did William Henry Hunt, who according to Ruskin 'painted mossy banks for five-and-twenty years, without ever caring to know a sphagnum from a polypody' – an attitude which Beatrix did not share.

The early twentieth century produced several fine fungus artists, among them women such as Constance Margaret Drummond Hay of Perthshire and, a generation after Beatrix, Mary Emily Eaton. Her paintings of *ca.* 1912–26 illustrate other people's work. She is one of the few (apart from Potter) capable of drawing fungi as three-dimensional objects. Though her backgrounds are vestigial, she makes notes on habitat; the composition is still a little stiff.

Nearly half a century before Beatrix Potter, Ruskin was subscribing to the limited edition (in 100 copies) of *Illustrations of British Mycology* (1847; 1855), a handsome chromo-lithographed work by Mrs A. M. Hussey. Mrs Hussey, who corresponded with Berkeley, was ahead of her time both artistically and scientifically, providing variant names and derivations, and showing structure. Few people can have known her work, and apparently not the Potters.

Beatrix was to discover fungi for herself.

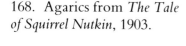

168. Agarics from *The Tale of Squirrel Nutkin*, 1903.

168

THE ARMITT PAINTINGS IN CONTEXT

It was natural that Beatrix should collect and draw her first fungi on holiday or at the houses of her relations: Woodcote, and Putney Park, where in 1891 she met her heroine Mrs Blackburn, the celebrated bird artist, and Camfield Place, her grandparents' house. Some of the earliest and latest fungus pictures were done when she was staying at Lingholm on Derwentwater, setting for *The Tale of Squirrel Nutkin* (*168*). Eastwood, Dunkeld, was the scene of much mycological activity in the autumn of 1893 (see pages 72 and 80); it was from here, also, that on 4 September she sent to young Noel Moore a picture story about Peter Rabbit, all unaware of its importance for her future life.

Predating the fungi are juvenile drawings already technically mature, including precise and lively studies of lizards and newts, strong crayon sketches of buildings, and fine-grained pen-and-inks of skulls (*170*). One of her

169. 'Long-eared bats disputing with a common bat for possession of the roosting place, drawn from tame animals.' Beatrix drew bats and insects as well as fungi at Camfield Place.

169

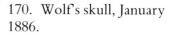

170

170. Wolf's skull, January 1886.

171. Boar-fish, Weymouth, 1895.

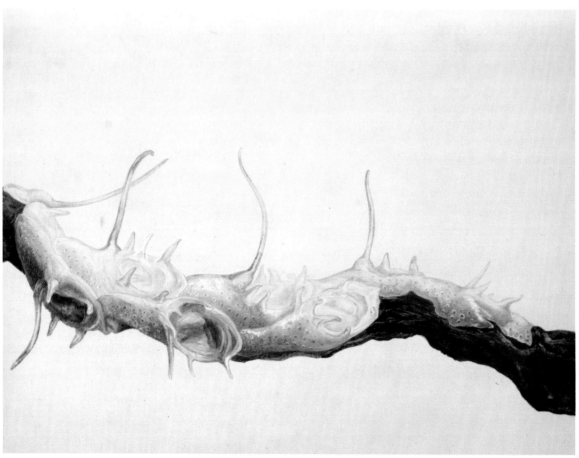

171

first-known microscopic works is of a colony of zooids on seaweed (*172*). The shore-hunting rage of a previous generation, fuelled by Philip Gosse and part of a more general passion for nature, left its traces in various other marine studies. Fish, with their variety of lustre and colour, seemed to William Henry Hunt ideal subjects for the artist. Beatrix's boar-fish (*171*) is comparable in quality with her fungi.

Most of her other microscopic drawing dates from 1886–87: insects and spiders, the wing-scales of butterflies and moths. In late 1895 Miss Caroline

172. Zooids, Eastbourne, 1886.

173. Painted Lady and Small Tortoiseshell butterflies with magnified wing-scales.

172

Painted Lady Butterfly.
Vanessa Cardui.
Scales on lower side of wing highly magnified.

Small Tortoise-shell Butterfly.
Vanessa Urticae
Scales on upper side of wing highly magnified.

174

174. *Cystoderma carcharias*,
Newlands, October 1901: a
late example.

175. 'Trial lithograph',
April 1896. Beatrix doubted
if these lithographs were 'of
any educational value,
because they were not drawn
with design'.

Martineau commissioned a set of lithographed
plates. Only the Sheet Web Spider (see page 29)
and Privet Hawk Moth survive, and a 'trial run'
of miscellaneous items which includes four
views of fungi.

Her fungus painting spans the years
1887–1901, reaching a peak in 1893–97; but the
archaeology and fossils absorbed her for a few
months only, between 1894 and 1895.

The Drawing Society to which she submitted
still lifes and flower studies, gardens and landscapes
seems to have been kept in ignorance of her scientific
occupations. A letter to Walter Gaddum (6 March 1897)
has a little sketch of fungi, which she planned to put in a
book one day – a hope still alive in 1905 (page 134). After
1900 the fungi had almost stopped 'coming up' – but she
still occasionally examined an individual plant in as much
detail as the fungi (*219*). In 1904, however, she had
returned to the fossils: 'I have been working very
industriously drawing fossils at the museum, upon the
theory that a change of work is the best sort of rest!'

175

Only rarely does she use fungi decoratively or whimsically, or in her backgrounds. They feature, as one would expect, mainly in earlier works (a dark-textured 'Red Riding Hood' design, the unpublished 1905 Book of Rhymes), as well as in *Squirrel Nutkin*, the only 'Tale' to

176. Illustration for 'Little Red Riding Hood' with ferns in the wall and Mycena-like fungi in the foreground.

176

include mushrooms in its autumnal setting – aptly, since squirrels eat them. Though less at the forefront of her mind by then, fungi appeared in 'The Oakmen' (1916) and *The Fairy Caravan* (1929), where bracket fungi are illustrated and unidentified toadstools play an active part in the plot. Her other subjects however, zoological or botanical, are continually recycled in the fantasy work, and especially in the Tales, whose success perhaps consoled her a little for her rejection by the academic establishment.

177. Bracket fungi in *The Fairy Caravan*, 1929.

177

178. The grassy tussocks from her fungus studies reappear in *The Tale of Mr. Jeremy Fisher,* 1906.

178

Three tales in particular reflect her knowledge of flora, fauna and habitat. *Squirrel Nutkin* is flora-rich; *Mr. Jeremy Fisher's* cast includes frog, fish, newt and tortoise, water beetle and water vole. Insects and spiders scuttle through *Mrs. Tittlemouse's* corridors.

Fairy-ring mushrooms can be sinister or benign (pages 131, 132); the fungi of her fantasy have their kindlier side too. 'The Mushrooms' from the 1905 Book of Rhymes hop and dance in 'the merry moon-light': dance was a favourite motif, and a sense of movement pervades her work. For the headpiece, a mushroom's natural features are cleverly metamorphosed into a little face with a fringe of hair above and a frilled ruff below, peeping out from under a 'mushroom hat'. Its border was to be 'clover, grass and button mushrooms, all brown'. The Victorians had a tendency to anthropomorphise – animal, vegetable or mineral.

'The Toads' Tea Party' (*179*), also from the Book of Rhymes, was originally envisaged with flatter fungi, and more of them:

179. 'The Toads' Tea Party', *ca*. 1905: paddocks and paddock stools.

179

> If acorn cups were tea-cups
>> What should we have to drink?
> Oh honey-dew for sugar
>> In a cuckoo-pint of milk,
> Set out upon a toadstool
>> On a cloth of cob-web silk,
> With pats of witches' butter
>> And a tansey cake, I think!

The tansy cake stands on the toadstool table, and the 'stools' are part of a bracket fungus. 'Witches' Butter' too is a fungus, *Exidia glandulosa*, black of course.

'Honey-dew' refers to the exudate of the ergot fungus (actually ingested by the guests in *The Tale of Mrs. Tittlemouse* – a private joke). Here composition conforms with subject: a rounded vignetted outline echoes the fungus shapes.

180. The black fungus *Exidia glandulosa*, known as Witches' Butter.

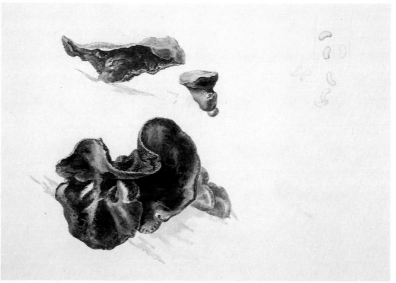

180

Fungi flourish on death and decay; to Beatrix –
incongruously yet perhaps symbolically – they seemed
alive and magical, and populated her consciousness as
much as the animals. 'I cannot tell what possesses me
with the fancy that they laugh and clap their hands,
especially the little ones that grow in troops and
rings amongst dead leaves in the woods. I suppose
it is the fairy rings, the myriads of fairy fungi
that start into life in autumn woods'
(*The Journal of Beatrix Potter*,
17 November 1896).

181. *Spathularia flava*,
Dunkeld, August 1895: fungi
semi-camouflaged among
leaves.

182. *Lactarius scrobiculatus*,
September 1900.

181

182

A SURVEY OF SUBJECT AND TECHNIQUE

Science goes hand in hand with imagination in Beatrix Potter's earliest art. Already a serious naturalist at the age of nine, she recorded in her own words the feeding habits of caterpillars; in her journal she speculated on the comparative evolution of fossils and fungi. Later, and sometimes for publication, she made more formal notes; her writings are vividly visual, notably in 'A Walk Amongst the Funguses' (pages 78, 82, 133). Thoroughly professional in her science, she aimed at analysis and accuracy. She visited the Natural History Museum not long after its move to South Kensington, to draw stuffed animals and to study insects and fossils. Like Jemima Blackburn (an earlier youthful dissector of dead animals) she was 'one of the last generation that did not see art and science as mutually exclusive; rather science provided a firmer foundation for aesthetic response' (Rob Fairley).[1] Drawing an object helps one to understand it; Beatrix was always determined to take things apart and analyse them – like the modern horseshoe lent her by Tom Squire, owner of the Roman artefacts which she borrowed to draw in the winter of 1894–95 (page 54).

183. Studies of horseshoes lent by Tom Squire, 'probably modern, and experimental'.

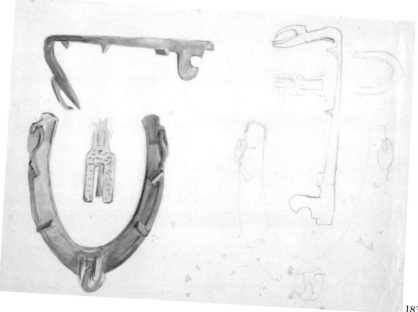

183

[1] *Jemima: The Paintings and Memoirs of a Victorian Lady* Edited and with an Introduction by Robert Fairley, Canongate Publishing Ltd, 1988.

184. The curves of pots
explored: a study in solidity,
light and shade.

184

'Struck by the bad taste' of much
Roman art, she none the less records
these man-made objects as lovingly
as the fungi; they inspired some of
her finest work. The artefacts are
seen in plan and elevation and from
different angles (*48*). Scale is indicated,
missing parts marked with a dotted
line, and potters' marks recorded
(*46*). The drawings are not just
inventories – unlike the flat outlines
of contemporary publications such as
Petrie's, or the *British Archaeological Association Journal*.
Even the elegant plates of Price's *Roman Antiquities* (1873)
are merely workmanlike in comparison. Beatrix had the
amateur's freedom from professional inhibition, and
could imaginatively mix different categories of object in
interesting juxtapositions of shape and colour, exploring
convexities and concavities, smoothness and solidity (*53,
184*).

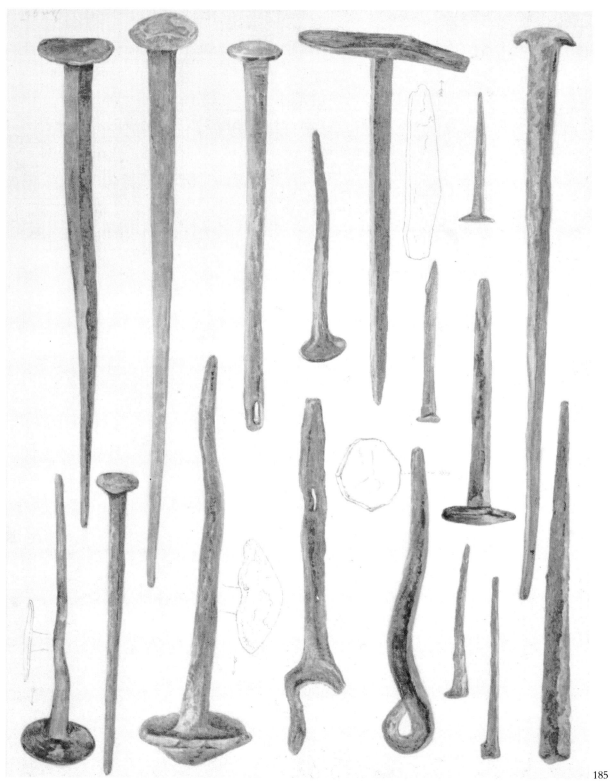

185

The size of the images can be surprising, and the feeling of depth. In hard–edged Pre-Raphaelite style, they have an uncanny sharpness almost hallucinogenic, like acrylics in its effect. These pictures are as accurate as photographs, by then much used in professional archaeology – yet they are so much more.

The tactile quality too is striking. Rusty flaking iron, its surface like mottled fabric, grates on the skin; areas of wear are indicated by a thinner application of paint (*186*). The knobby hardness of the shoe leathers seems 'a fossil record of their owner' (John Gavin, *Quarto*, July 1990; *187*).

Fossils first became an enthusiasm at Dalguise, though Beatrix apparently did not record her finds until the 1890s. At Coldstream in 1894 she was 'overtaken' by

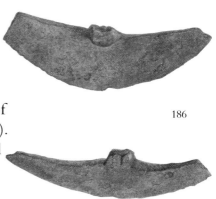

186

186. Two views of a turf cutter, July 1895.

187. Shoe leather: three views, 1895.

185. A comparative study of nails, 1895, showing different elevations and angles.

187

fossils as well as fungi. She read up her geology: 'I have found out which stones to split and how to use a cold chisel' but 'I find it better not to expect or worry much about geology'. Geology, a study still in its infancy, bridged science and art, as did botanical drawing. Rocks have a special appeal for draughtsmen: their complicated textures intrigued Victorian artists like Ruskin, and John Brett (*The Glacier of Rosenlaui*, 1856).

'Art is hidden in nature and he who can draw it out possesses it,' said Dürer – who in 1503 painted the first study of plants in their natural setting ('The Great Piece of Turf'). The Pre-Raphaelites too wanted to draw what was there; Dürer was their model. To Ruskin, who championed the Pre-Raphaelites, artistic and scientific truth seemed the same. Beatrix Potter, though rude about Ruskin and the later Pre-Raphaelites, approved of their original ideas. Like Jemima Blackburn, she acknowledged their influence. 'When I was young it was still the fashion to admire Pre-Raphaelites' and 'their somewhat niggling but absolutely genuine admiration for copying natural details did certainly influence me' – as did their attempts at an exact re-creation of the effects of light.

In such a climate, photography was naturally much in vogue. 'Mr Millais says all the artists use photographs now', and himself relied on Rupert Potter's excellent portrait and landscape backgrounds. Beatrix inherited her father's heavy discarded cameras, but in 1895 she had a new one with a 'lovely mahogany complexion', and photographed fungi, ferns and fossils. The Armitt Library has several examples by both father and daughter. Photographs, however, are often less practical than record drawings, which can isolate the relevant and exclude the irrelevant. A photograph, too, can capture only a single moment, but a painting evolves over time. And even the best photographs can be no substitute for the artist's personal vision.

The fossils are painted in a spectrum of greys rather reminiscent of photographs. They are treated more academically than the fungi, which are rarely shown in regimented layouts (*100, 114, 208*). Unlike fungi, fossils did not deteriorate; they could be found one year and drawn the next.

Fungi, with their extraordinary shapes and colours, had originally attracted Beatrix as objects. Oddly enough, she at first found them difficult to draw. Some early attempts seem washy and undefined (*63, 64*), though her insects, for example, are never imprecise. She insisted on working with fresh models whenever possible (*73*), and was later to criticise the closet naturalists who made 'theories out of dried specimens' (pages 108, 110). (Certainly it is hard to create the illusion of three dimensions from dried models.) To her exacting eye, very few artists saw the beauty of nature unadorned, or its unity. 'What we call highest and lowest in nature are both equally perfect. A willow bush is as beautiful as the *human form divine.*' She criticised bad colour and defective drawing, berating even Millais for inaccuracy. In 1921 she recommended the young Sylvie Heelis to study nature, take pains, and above all be thorough.

Practice matched theory. Making rapid pencil sketches on the spot, or recording a later discovery, often on the reverse of another drawing, she noted condition and

188. Jew's Ear (*Hirneola auricula-judae*) at Sidbury Camp, Devon, April 1898.

188

191. *Agaricus bisporus*, the cultivated mushroom, with the wild variety (*Agaricus campestris*), Woodcote, August 1897.

192. Shaggy Parasol Mushroom (*Lepiota rhacodes*), Kinnaird, Dunkeld, September 1893.

189. Cowslip plants in grass, ?1904.

190. *Cystoderma amianthinum*, Tomgarrow, Strathbraan, October 1893.

colour, habitat and habit. Exact portrayal of growth, whether of fungi or trees, demanded close observation (*73, 90, 91, 188, 218, 226*). Trees interested her both scientifically and imaginatively: 'I did so many careful botanical studies in my youth, it became easy for me to draw twigs . . . little details like that add to the reality of a picture' (letter to Fruing Warne, 5 August 1920). She seems more conscious than her contemporaries of the significance of habitat – as in the accurate and all-important backdrops of her book illustrations, where only the landscapes are idealised, never the natural history.

Early subjects often lack background; even in later examples, the setting may be absent, or barely hinted at (*93, 161, 200*). The fungi nestle among grass and dead leaves, pine needles and fern, squat in lichen and moss (*33, 61, 92, 158, 174, 190, 196, 223, 226*) or spring up from grassy tussocks, like her cowslips (*60*). The turf is often uprooted, or the fungi lie tumbled and broken, their underground parts laid bare (*76, 80, 192*). The background may be important in its own right: a pattern of leaves (*84*), or strands of grass like a scribble across the surface of the cap (*83*). Damage and disease are always shown (*33, 106, 159, 204, 225*): it was an unofficial convention in amateur flower painting never to disguise fading or other deterioration (Mabey, *The Flowering of Kew*).

189

190

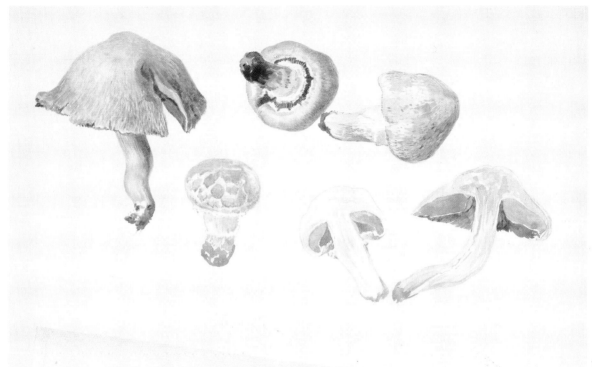

191

192

159

193

194

A subject may stand out from its setting (*81, 82, 193, 229*), or be well-camouflaged, unfocussed and undefined among the more clearly delineated substrate (*61, 62, 181, 218*). Specimens of every size encrust tree-trunks, twigs and bark, sprouting out in clusters or clinging on leech-like (*91, 126, 130, 167, 194*). Fungi grow on broom, on heather at Woodcote or cowdung at Esthwaite, in a rubbish heap at Wray Castle or a coal cellar in London's Finborough Road (*200, 211*).

Conscious or unconscious, there is always the urge to arrange – to make a picture. Complete objectivity is impossible in scientific illustration; the brain always selects, imposing its own order. Some compositions are as much artist's impressions as bio-records (*77, 80, 81, 96*). Fly Agaric seems a fashionable set-piece, possibly done as a present (*195*). It unites her early opaque method with a later command of texture, and uncharacteristically brings together plants of different habitat and season: fungus, lichen, moss and fern.

193. Scarlet Elf Cup (*Sarcoscypha coccinea*), ?1897. The deep russet pink stands out from the blue-green substrate of moss and lichen.

194. *Gloeophyllum sepiarium*, Inver, October 1893.

195

195. Fly Agaric (*Amanita muscaria*) with Polypody fern, beech leaves, mosses and lichen *Peltigera canina, ca.* 1890.

Individual specimens stand out with exquisite clarity; they are never flat (*79, 93, 104*). Some, like the fossils, have shadows to give them solidity (*94, 198*); in others the shadow is faint, or non-existent (*83, 93, 208*). Where 'study sections' or other diagrams are included, they are usually isolated from the pictorial component (*82, 113*) or removed to another sheet (*97, 123, 155*). (Even before Charlie McIntosh's letter, from time to time she did attempt to draw both sections and gills (*62, 137*).) Where sections are part of the group, care is taken not to unbalance the composition (*79, 196, 199, 226*). Naturally lighter in tone, they are kept to one side or in the background (*34, 86, 106, 107, 197, 202, 214*); and where the section is separate, it still follows the movement of the composition (*158*).

196. Slimy Milk Cap (*Lactarius blennius*), Hatchednize Wood, Coldstream, September 1894.

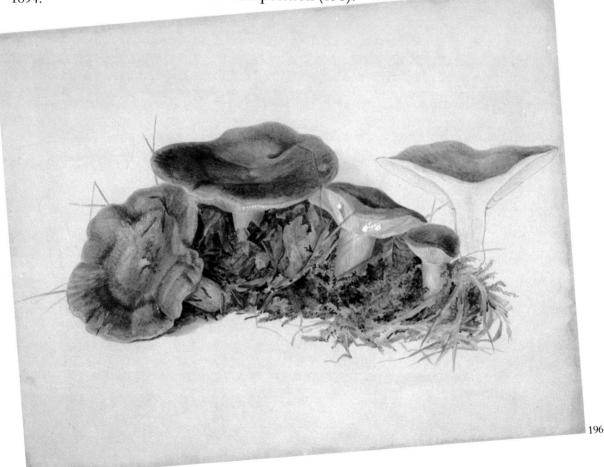

196

197

197. Parasol Mushroom
(*Lepiota procera*), Lennel,
Coldstream, August 1894.
The large specimen
dominates the sheet, while
diagrammatic elements lie
discreetly behind.

198

198. The Blusher (*Amanita
rubescens*), Dunkeld, August
1893. A curve of mushrooms
used as a compositional
device.

This sense of movement is increased by the structuring
of the composition: a dynamic equilibrium seen also in
the book pictures. An internal curve gives interest to a
compact central cluster (*213*); a sinuous line swerves from
front left to back right (*198*); or a strong diagonal sweeps
across the sheet (*188*). Asymmetry provides interest and
helps to balance the page (*77, 81*).

199. *Amanita excelsa*, Lennel, July 1894.

Colour disposition is another subtle balancing instrument: extra intensity of colour at one side adds to the asymmetric effect (*81, 96*). Weight conspires with height, where the taller figure has a heavier base (*77*).

In one especially pleasing agglomeration of shapes the weight is concentrated below (*199*). More ethereal fungi seem to float (*200*), flying off the page, as in an unconventional view of *Lepiota konradii* (*201*), cut off at the edge.

Occasionally the layout is less 'artistic' and the subjects treated purely as specimens, as with the mosses, which perhaps captured

200. *Lepiota friesii* on a rubbish heap at Wray Castle, September 1895.

201. *Lepiota konradii*, Sawrey, September 1896.

199

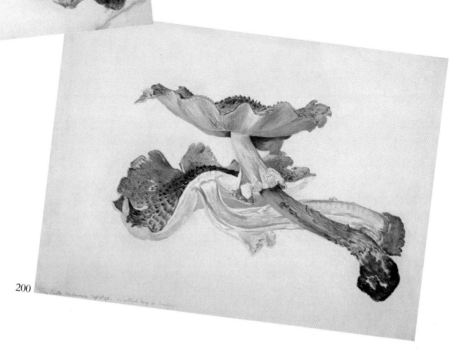

200

her imagination less (*95, 113, 137, 146*). Some sheets have simply been cut down or cropped (*113, 201*); a few appear intentionally informal (*203*). One 'Old Man of the Woods' (*73*) is a tighter composition than its companion piece (*231*). But more often, format is fitted to fungus subject: leggier individuals, emphatically vertical, are shown in portrait format, and overlapping clusters in 'landscape' (*98, 192, 197, 203, 226*). A double portrait is almost invariably a happy marriage (*67, 72*). And the various elements of the composition, often interspersed with microscopic details, may be moved about to suit the page, like the arrangements of artefacts or the lithographs (*130*). All Beatrix Potter's work shows this sense of equilibrium and design.

202. The Prince (*Agaricus augustus*), Dunkeld, August 1893.

202

201

203. *Suillus bovinus*. A painterly, more impressionistic treatment (probably unfinished).

203

The angle of vision varies from high to low, from microscope lens to hand-lens. The pine cone (*205*) is viewed at eye-level, so that one can almost see between the scales (the loose scale is a nice touch). This image too is unexpectedly large, with a powerful and stereoscopically three-dimensional effect. The tiniest fungi are contrasted with larger varieties (*76, 115, 126, 129, 157, 204, 209, 220*); different sizes of the same species set one another off, from small buttons to the large flat caps of fully-grown fruiting bodies (*95, 96, 102, 137, 198, 206*).

204

204. Stump Puff Ball (*Lycoperdon pyriforme*), Lingholm, September 1897.

205. A pine cone, 1895, drawn in the technique of Beatrix Potter's best fungus and fossil studies.

206. *Amanita excelsa,* Holehird, August 1895.

205

206

Beatrix Potter's fungi, like her animals, are drawn in different poses: in rows or layers, huddled or fatly tumbled, or in palely sinister heaps (*76, 80, 84, 203, 211*). W. H. K. Findlay in his book (pages 55, 56) groups her studies of four types of stalk: long, thick, lateral, absent. *Psathyrella* (*207*) combines crossing stems both curved and straight.

207

207. *Psathyrella* species, Dunkeld, October 1894.

208. *Mycena galericulata*, Sawrey, September 1896.

208

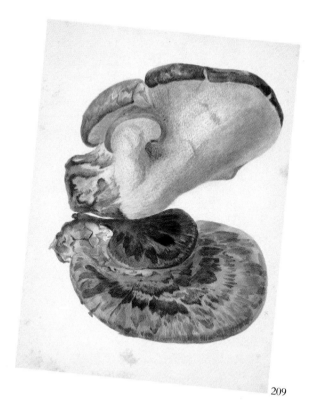

209

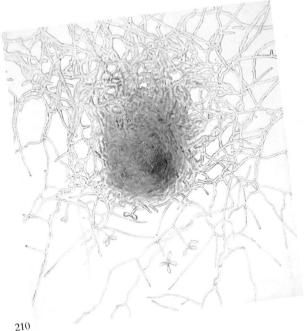

210

211

209. Dryad's Saddle
(*Polyporus squamosus*),
Dunkeld, July 1894.

210. A spidery mass of
mycelium magnified × 600,
January 1898.

211. *Pleurotus ulmarius*,
November 1893.

212

She revels in strange growths and forms (*60, 67, 80, 159, 209*): elegant feathery strands of moss, sheet-engulfing spiders' webs of mycelium, edges broken or wavy, curly pancakes or crinkled poppadums (*61, 106, 153, 180, 203, 210, 211*), caps hollow-lipped, cup-shaped, conical or like pansies (*68, 105, 126, 154, 229*). Common mushrooms are considered from above and then from below (*161, 162*); other examples show the underside in close-up (*212, 217, 222*); sections especially are often inverted (*79, 81, 83*).

Experience in relief modelling helped her to study her subjects from all angles, as a sculptor surveys a human head for a portrait. She relished the solid curvaceousness of bun-shaped boletes, like soft hats or piled-up pebbles (*76, 80, 83*). And her handling of light, shade and perspective increases the sculptural effect.

212. Horse Mushroom (*Agaricus arvensis*), Cat Bells, Keswick, September 1897.

213. *Leccinum melanea.* The stems are snake-like in shape as well as texture.

215. *Sarcodon imbricatum,* Murthly, Perthshire, August 1894.

Texture delighted her: caps craggy and cratered, prickly or scaly (*74, 75, 192, 197, 214, 215, 225, 231*), crisp or slimy (*96, 223*), stalks marked like snake-skin (*77, 213*), soft creases and folds (*61, 196*), the granular yet velvety feel of Dead Man's Fingers (*218*). As with the artefacts and fossils, the appeal is to our sense of touch – there seems an almost tactile contact with the image. The intricacies of gills she found difficult at first, but could soon manage skilfully with fine brush strokes, parallel or varied in shape and thickness. Some are deeply defined, others barely insinuated, according to the fall of light (*34, 86, 93, 111, 216, 217, 222*).

213

214

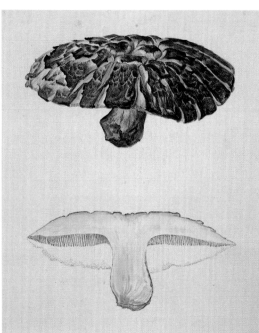

215

214. Parasol Mushroom (*Lepiota procera*) with cratered caps and stems.

216. *Tricholoma sulphureum*, Birgham, Coldstream, October 1894.

216

217. *Lepista* species, with a contemporary look, almost as if painted in acrylics.

217

218. Dead Man's Fingers (*Xylaria polymorpha*) on laurel, August 1896.

218

direct light
from this side

Sweet Bay Tree

against the light

the veins in the leaf are slightly
transparent —

There has been no sunshine & evergreen leaves show very little
transparent light without it

219. Spray of Sweet Bay,
1900.

220. Beef Steak Fungus
(*Fistulina hepatica*),
Eastwood, Dunkeld, August
1893.

Textural quality is achieved through the management of light and shade – an important ingredient of Beatrix Potter's art. She was fascinated by the reflections of light, and the re-creation of light with colour. 'Sunlight & shadow' is the title of a barn interior; a study of bay leaves (*219*) is inscribed with arrows showing the direction of the light, and the observation: 'There has been no sunshine & evergreen leaves show very little transparent light without it.' Glowing colour and glossy highlights, serving as focus, attract the eye in Bunsen burner flame and fire or in Fly Agaric (*80, 82, 195*).

The colour of fungi – sometimes startling, always subtle – is as much of a challenge to the painter as their texture: pinky-reds and russets (*80, 82, 193, 220*), yellows from cool lemon to rich gold (*32, 85, 157*), blues or metallic greens as bright as her Amazon parrot (*126, 166, 224; 221*). Lighter hues need the contrast of dark-toned backgrounds (*94, 223*). Fine distinctions between shades of white and cream (*34, 199, 211*) are handled as successfully as the gamut of greys and browns,

221

221. Orange-winged
Amazon Parrot, 1890, in
profile and 'in full dress'.

222. *Russula nigricans*,
Eastwood, Dunkeld, August
1893.

222

223

223. *Clitopilus prunulus*,
Hatchednize Wood,
Coldstream, August 1894.
The crisp-edged pale fungi
nestle among rich brown
leaves.

224. Parrot Toadstool
(*Hygrocybe psittacina*),
Coldstream, August 1894.
As vividly green as its
Amazon namesake (221).

224

translucent or dense (*93, 96, 100, 104, 105, 124, 167*). Particularly diverse in colour are the fungi growing on wood: green-staining, purple or deep turquoise, soft brown or shell-like pink (*126, 188, 218*). Grass, sap-green or blue-green, gives prominence to the central subject, as a grey background flatters a foreground in lemon and pink (*60, 107; 80*). Damage and decay can affect colour (*79, 159, 225*); a small hole in the cap even acts as focal point (*199, 204*).

'An Even Tint is not in Nature; it produces Heaviness' (William Blake). Her perception of colour is as remarkable as her ability to reproduce it (*80, 179*). For tree, stone and toadstool as for the short glossy fur of mammals and bees, tiny pointillistic strokes impart brilliance, lustre and bloom (*55, 81, 135, 171, 226, 227*).

225. *Boletus versicolor*, Derwent Bay Wood, August 1897.

226. *Psathyrella* species, Ford, Northumberland, August 1894. Lanky crossing stems on moss-covered rock.

225

226

227

227. From 'Three Little Mice', *ca*. 1892. As with *Lepiota konradii* (201), the composition runs off the edge of the sheet.

The description of intricate surfaces and intense hues demands pure tints, applied thickly and drily with a good quality brush. There may be more graphite underpainting than is obvious to the naked eye; pencil hatchings beneath the paint create an illusion of depth, as in 'The Three Little Mice' (*227*).

Unfinished examples reveal her technique of lightly sketching in the composition in pencil (*99, 103, 108, 191*). The background was completed first, before the fungus (*228*), a method adopted for her landscapes with figures. Some examples are in line and wash, or include pen-and-ink outlines, probably done in reed pen, which produces a fine hard line.

Experimentation, and a constant striving for perfection, led her to draw and redraw – and not only the fungi: many fantasy drawings and book pictures too survive in several versions. The lively, fluid narrative line so characteristic of her more familiar works developed in parallel with this very different sort of art. There is not the same opportunity for experimentation in natural history illustration, where to a large extent subject must dictate style.

The Armitt fungi, mainly painted on thin card, are more uniform in appearance than her other work (partly on thin paper which cockled; the book pictures on a variety of papers, some unsatisfactory in quality). Two versions of the same fungus, however, are painted on different supports (*73, 231*); and occasionally a darker colour is chosen to serve as ground. A smooth surface with little texture is best suited to the fine detail of botanical drawing.

228. An unfinished study, the fungus still uncoloured.

229. Conical Wax Cap (*Hygrocybe conica*), Holehird, September 1895.

228

229

IN CONCLUSION

The Armitt paintings, protected from light in portfolios (pages 46–7), have kept their fresh colours: only a few, such as *Amanita phalloides* (*89, 153*), have faded. They were never framed: Beatrix Potter did not work for exhibition. In spite of early failures of confidence, she was encouraged by the example of other women artists: Rosa Bonheur and Angelica Kauffmann, Lady Waterford and Jemima Blackburn. In 1920, she wondered 'how I ever drew so much and so well, while I could see'. She always knew that the fungus illustrations were good – but very few people had ever seen them. She wished all her paintings to be given to some public collection, not sold.

So many botanical drawings are correct but lifeless, lacking (as Millais said) the 'divine spark': many people could draw, but not everyone was gifted with observation – and only a few had inspiration. According to Ruskin, W. H. Hunt could draw a mug 'to the uttermost muggy', and make it stand for something else. Frederick Walker's *Mushrooms and Fungi* (1868) were 'lovely in colour and showing a kind of divination as well as imitative skill' (Martin Hardie). Both these statements could apply equally well to Beatrix Potter's scientific work. Intensity of vision and mastery of technique together communicate shape and texture, colour and light.

Beatrix Potter's fungi seem real, fresh, and alive in their settings. They are portraits with personality: one can see them, touch them, and almost smell them. Reacting with her senses and her intellect to the world around her, she appeals to our senses and our intellect.

Most significantly, she was her own illustrator. As both artist and author, she brought an extra dimension to her books. As both artist and scientist, she brought something extra to her natural history. She too, like the Armitt sisters, 'sowed that other minds might reap'.

230. *Fissidens adianthoides.*

231. Old Man of the Woods (*Strobilomyces floccopus*), Eastwood, September 1893. It is drawn on a different paper from its duplicate on page 72.

230

Strobilomyces Strobilaceus. Sept 3d 93 Dunkeld.

231

INDEX

Figures in *italics* refer to plates.

Index of Names:

Fungi, Algae, Lichens

Parentheses indicate brief references only.

Agaricus genus, 58
Agaricus spp., 58, 92–3, 97, 107, 118, 148, 149–50; *168, 177*
A. arvensis: Horse Mushroom, *212*
A. augustus: The Prince, *202*
A. aureus var. *vahlii*, see *Phaeolepiota aurea*
A. bisporus (Common or Cultivated Mushroom), 58, 118–19, 135, 169; *161, 162, 191*
A. (Omphalia) campanella, see *Omphalina pseudoandrosacea*
A. campestris: Common or Field Mushroom, *160, 191*
A. cortinarius turmalis, see under *Cortinarius cinnamomeobadius*
A. decastes, see *Lyophyllum decastes*
A. fragrans, see *Boletus fragrans*
A. hypnorus, see *Galerina hypnorum*
A. imbricatus, see *Tricholoma imbricatum*
A. lenticularis, see *Limacella guttata*
A. longicaudus, see *Hebeloma longicaudum*
A. mitis, see *Panellus mitis*
A. paedidus, see *Lyophyllum decastes*
A. personatus, see *Lepista saeva*
A. pleurotus ulmarius, see *Pleurotus ulmarius*
A. portentosus, see *Tricholoma portentosum*
A. spadiceus, see *Psathyrella spadicea*
A. squarrosus, see *Pholiota squarrosa*
A. terreus, see *Tricholoma sciodes*
A. vaccinus, see *T. vaccinum*
A. variabilis, see *Crepidotus variabilis*
A. velutipes, see *Flammulina velutipes*
Aleurodiscus amorphus (*Corticium amorphum*), 107, 108–9, 110, 118; *57, 117(a), 125*
Amanita citrina: False Death Cap, 80; *89*

A. excelsa, 199, 206
A. muscaria: Fly Agaric, 59, 160, 172; *195*
A. phalloides: The Death Cap, 130, 180; *153*
A. rubescens: The Blusher, *198*
Ascobolus sp., 103

Boletus spp., 73–4, 77–8, 95, 107, 120, 121, 133, 169; see also *Leccinum; Strobilomyces; Suillus*
B. badius: Bay Bolete, 75, 77, 133; *78, 159*
B. bovinus, see *Suillus bovinus*
B. calopus (*pachypus*), 71, 75; *80*
B. chrysenteron: Red-cracked Bolete, 71, 73; *74*
B. cyanescens, see *Gyroporus cyanescens*
B. edulis: Edible Bolete, Cep or Penny Bun, 77; *83*
B. erythropus: Red Leg or Red-stalked Bolete, 75, 133; *79*
B. fragrans (*Agaricus fragrans*): Funnel Cap, 67
B. granulatus, see *Suillus granulatus*
B. laricinus, see *S. aeruginascens*
B. luridus, 71, (75)
B. luteus, see *Suillus luteus*
B. pachypus, see *B. calopus*
B. porosporus (*subtomentosus*): Downy Bolete, 71, 73; *75*
B. scaber, (97); see *Leccinum scabrum*
B. subtomentosus, see *B. porosporus*
B. versicolor, 225
B. versipellis, see *Leccinum versipelle* bracket fungus, 148, 150; *177, 179*
Bulgaria inquinans: Black Bulgar, 106; *123–4*

Cantherellula umbonata (*Cantherellus umbonatus*), 81, 83; *92*
Cantharellus cibarius: Chanterelle, 60, 130, 133; *32, 64*

C. umbonatus, see *Cantharellula umbonata*
Chlorociboria aeruginascens (*Chlorosplenium aeruginosum*): Green Wood Cup, 107, 110; *126*
Chlorosplenium aeruginosum, see *Chlorociboria aeruginascens*
Chondrostereum purpureum (*Stereum purpureum*): Silver-leaf Fungus, 67, 70
Chroogomphus maculatus, see *Gomphidius maculatus*
C. rutilus (*Gomphidius viscidus*): Pine Spike Cap, 95, 96; *111*
Cladonia spp. ('Reindeer' lichens), 113, 116; *132–3*
C. pyxidata: Pixie Cup, 116; *128, 131*
Claviceps purpurea: Ergot, 151
Clitocybe nebularis (*Lepista nebularis*): Clouded Agaric or Clouded Clitocybe, *33*
C. prunulus: The Miller, *223*
Collybia sp., 80; *88*
C. butyracea: Butter Cap or Greasy Tough Shank, 80; *88*
C. dryophila: Russet Shank, 60; *62*
Coprinus micaceus: Glistening Ink Cap, 102; *121*
Coriolus versicolor: Many-zoned or Green-zoned Polypore, *55, 166*
Corticium amorphum, see *Aleurodiscus amorphus*
Cortinarius sp., 59, 71, 81, 85, 87, 90–91, 92, 93; *95*
C. ? cinnamomeobadius (*cinnamomeus*, *Agaricus cortinarius turmalis*): Cinnamon Cortinarius, (90–91), 92, 93; *105*
C. multiformis, 91
C. turmalis, see *C. cinnamomeobadius*
Crepidotus sp. (inc. *Agaricus variabilis*), 58, 66, 67, 68; *70*
C. mollis, 68
cup fungi, 98–9, 116; *134*; see also *Bulgaria inquinans; Lachnellula* spp.; *Peziza* spp.; *Poculum* spp.
Cystoderma amianthinum, 190
C. carcharias, 174